Not All Witches Ride On Broomsticks

Kerry M Hill

ISBN: 9798620550616

DEDICATION

I am dedicating this book to my Wonderful Husband and two Children, who support me tirelessly.

CONTENTS

ACKNOWLEDGMENTS

Those that I love, all the people who have been through a hard time, and those facing uncertain times.

1 PRELUDE

Have you ever had a feeling before something big happened in your life, a feeling that you knew what was coming before it had become a reality? Maybe you had a bad feeling about an event or a person that turned out to be right? Or, you've unsurely followed an instinct that led you to a better place, despite your reservations? I think we can all say we've been there. Some of us may have had more in-depth insight than others, but almost all of us can recall having had an experience that we wish we'd followed or thank that we trusted. They say a woman's intuition should always be relied on, that it is the most undervalued instinct we have as human beings. But what if it were something that we all had, not just women, but men and children too. What if it's not even intuition at all…

……………………………………………………………

I'd only just arrived here but already it was obvious I was a bit different. I stood out from most of the crowd. I was sat on the London Underground, not for the first time, but for the first time on my own, making my way into the City Centre. Well, not Zone 1 but still central enough to be considered the city centre. Mammy had made me a packed lunch for my journey, which was sat on my lap, and this was clearly the first clue that I wasn't a 'Londoner'. They were all stood around with their trendy coffee cups, reusable of course, and boxed Quinoa and Kale vegan salad in biodegradable packaging, while I wasn't even sure how to even pronounce quinoa even if I'd wanted to order one. In contrast I was sat there with Mammy's Corned Beef sandwiches, wrapped in tin foil, made using plain, old white bread. I tucked into my sandwich with gusto, but I could feel eyes watching me as I ate, and I looked up to see a man looking back at me. He was in his mid-twenties wearing a well-cut suit and a crisp, perfectly ironed, white shirt. His hair was slicked back and shiny, which matched his well-polished shiny black shoes, and his expression was one of bewilderment. I frowned at him to show that I'd noticed him staring at me, but still he continued in his confused and disapproving surveyal of me. Undeterred I turned my attention back to my lunch. I knew my journey wasn't too long and I wanted to eat my lunch quickly while I had somewhere to sit, and if I saved it until I arrived it would be too late for lunch, which could then throw out my whole dinner time routine. I pulled out my carton of Ribena and I prised open the rinsed-out tub from the local takeaway that Mammy had used for my chopped-up fruit, and continued with my lunch, forcing myself to ignore my rude spectator.

I ate quickly, so as not to risk too many germs lingering on my food. The tube was a busy thing, and all those close bodies breathing in the same warm, recycled air was a recipe for disaster. Especially for someone like me coming from the countryside and being used to clean air in abundance. That was one of the reasons my parents didn't want me coming to London, they thought it was unclean and unsafe. But I wanted an adventure, I told them, I wanted to spread my wings, and I could think of no better place to try and find my real self, or even a better version of me. I quickly finished my lunch and sat back, satisfied that my hunger had now subsided, and I decided it was my turn to people watch and started to look around at my fellow tube goers. There were people of all ages surrounding me, dressed in an array of outfits. The lady next to me was clearly well to do, as she was head to toe in designer outfits. Not that I'd had much experience with designer outfits to recognise them by sight, but in preparation for my move to the City I'd started perusing some of the fancy, glossy magazines from the Supermarket. Our local shop hadn't stocked them, there wasn't the demand the shopkeeper told me, and when supply outweighs demand it's a recipe for bankruptcy he'd told me, so I'd needed to get the bus once a week in to the Town to get the 'in vogue' literature that would help me become in season with the latest trends. I very much aspired to be one of those perfectly dressed and preened ladies, the ones that make people turn and watch as they pass by. A bit like the lady next to me. She was wearing a beautiful chequered shawl that I recognized as the Burberry pattern. Her boots were red on the bottom which showed they were Louboutin, and her trousers had DKNY embroidered on to the belt loops. Her outfit was completed with a Mulberry bag. I shuddered to think how much her outfit cost. I'm sure, from what I could remember seeing in the magazines, that her bag probably cost more than my Dad's car. I bet this lady never took a packed lunch with her, let alone ate it on public transport, but I was sure she definitely wouldn't have anybody eyeing her disdainfully. I must make a mental note, for my new, cool life, that packed lunches on trains is a big no-no. I continued to look around and spotted the man who had been watching me eat my lunch. He had now moved down the carriage to an empty seat and seemed to have been distracted from watching me any longer. Looking around there were plenty of others just like him. Standard black or navy suits, with white shirts and an array of ties. All of them super polished and super slick desperately jabbing at their phones willing for some signal so they could get back to being important. Bankers, I imagined. Opposite me sat a young girl who had a clear affinity for the colour black. Everything about her was black - her clothes, her bag, her make-up, her nail varnish. She was gothic, but in a cool sort of way. She oozed attitude, and a no-care-in-the-world demeanour, but she was still well put together with matching accessories and perfectly blow-dried hair, black of course. I looked down at my own outfit. I was wearing Mammy's parker coat, as it had been raining when I'd left the house and I'd already packed my waterproof in my suitcase. It was a little bit too big for me and hung down to my knees. It also wasn't the best colour in the world, it was a kind of khaki green, that had faded over time. Mammy had insisted on keeping it, it's sturdy and washes out easily she'd said. But it had certainly seen better days. I must remember to give it back to her at the earliest opportunity, it wouldn't be staying a part of the new me. Before I'd left for my new life, I had bought myself some new kitten heeled boots for everyday wear, as I'd seen them in an article that had described them as the 'perfect accessory to any outfit'. Apparently, they were comfortable and chic, just what I was looking for. One of the things I'd hoped for the new London me was to be more sophisticated and fashionable. But I hadn't worn my new boots today as I had to do quite a lot of walking with my suitcase, and as I wasn't used to wearing heels so I'd worried that I wouldn't quite cope in my new shoes very well. Instead, I had pulled on my old, comfy trainers, and laced them up tight in case of any looseness rubbing and causing blisters. The trainers themselves weren't completely unusual on this tube full of fashion forward individuals, it was more the way I was wearing them. I noticed that all of the other trainers seemed to have their laces hidden at the top, whereas mine were tied up, double looped even, proudly sat at the nape of the tongue. Maybe I'd Youtube a video later today on how to tie shoelaces so that they looked cool, I'm sure if I wore them in the right way my old trainers would be perfectly acceptable for casual wear. To the side of me two girls around my age were stood up and engaged in conversation, giggling and carefree. They were both wearing cropped jumpers, which I completely did not understand the point of, jumpers are for keeping warm and if it doesn't cover your whole torso it will not keep you warm. I'd already decided that cropped tops of any kind would be one trend I would not be following. Anyway, there they were wearing cropped jumpers and both of them were stretching up to hold on to the pole above them to steady themselves. There were plenty of seats around so I assumed that they had stood up on purpose to show off their toned mid-sections, as reaching up to the handrail had resulted in both of their tops riding higher than normal, and both of their flat stomachs were completely on show, along with most of their rib cage. I didn't really blame them, if my mid-section looked like theirs, I might be persuaded to show it off. Probably not, but maybe. I continued to survey the other passengers around and I also noted that my average size 12 body didn't seem to be the norm here. I say average, as I'd heard it was the UK average size for women these days, but it seemed to be a little bit large around these parts. Maybe I'd try to lose a couple of pounds over the next few weeks. I could probably leave the biscuits I had with my tea, although I'd always been partial to a dip in my sweet tea with a hobnob. But if I cut those out then that could save me some calories. I'd just have to limit myself to one a day with my bedtime hot milk – a treat. I could even take up some exercise. I'd read about these fitness classes that were all the craze in America and were just coming to London. They claimed to help you burn up to 600 calories in 30 minutes! That would certainly help my mid-section look a little less Jelly. I'd definitely have to look into that when I had settled in. New me, new body. So many people from my hometown thought I was a bit mad for wanting to come to London, especially when I had a readymade job at home with a business to take over eventually. It had been a really hard decision to make, I was unfamiliar with city life and thanks to living in a small village I felt like I was leaving a whole community behind. I couldn't explain to those around me why I wanted to leave, as I was fairly happy with my set up at home, but I had a fascination for learning and longed to study further, and part of me felt like life had a bit more to offer me. As much as I had tried to ignore it, the older I got the more I felt the nagging feeling that I needed to get out and find what I was really meant for in life, rather than just taking the easy option. So here I was, ready to grow and explore, albeit slightly sceptical that I'd made the right decision. The familiar screech of brakes broke me away from my thoughts. As the tube started pulling into my stop, I grabbed my bag and case and politely tried to excuse myself past the crowds.

'Excuse me, please can I get by?' I gently asked the bodies blocking my way.

Nobody moved. Maybe they didn't hear me?!

'Excuse me, please may I squeeze past?' I asked again, voice raised slightly.

Still nobody moved.

'Excuse me!' I shouted, almost frantic that I was going to miss my stop.

This time one man looked up from the book he was reading

and glanced at me. But just as quickly he went back to reading his book, and he had not moved an inch to allow me past. The tube doors started to close, and in panic I barged my way past people for the first time in my life and almost fell on to the platform. I looked back at the people that had stood in my way, just as the doors came together, and not one of them seemed to have even registered anyone or anything had shoved them out of their positions.

'Move!' A man shouted at me unexpectedly, and I jumped back against the wall to let the people past as I continued to stand a little confused and a little shaken.

'Huh!' I exclaimed aloud, 'Welcome to London!'.

2 INTRODUCTION

I was a regular girl as a child. I wasn't particularly attractive, although I wouldn't characterise myself as ugly either. I was what you'd describe as non-descript. The only part of me that stood out was my crazy hair – huge, great frizz of ginger, it wasn't curly although how I'd longed for it to be perfect shiny barrels of curls like you see in the adverts, but it never quite got to the beautiful hair I wished it would be. Over the years I'd wasted so much of my hard-earned pocket money on these 'miracle' frizz free products, yet my hair still stayed very much full of frizz. However, as I mentioned, it was the only thing that set me apart from all the other average girls growing up, with their freckled, slightly chubby faces and braced teeth. I accepted early on that I wasn't going to be one of life's beauties no matter how much money I spent buying products on a Saturday afternoon in Superdrug, and instead made a path for myself as a bit of a tomboy. I loved the outdoors anyway, I loved a bit of adventure and exploring, and my wild hair fitted in with my wild adventures. At least they seemed wild to me as a 10-year-old. Looking back, they weren't nearly as exciting as they'd seemed then, but it kept me busy and active – and most of all happy.

Life had always been quite a simple thing for me. I grew up in a picturesque, quaint, rural village somewhere in between London and Birmingham. It was a beautiful village, with lots of old cottages with traditional thatched roofs that all seemed to have a steep at the top. None of the houses were particular large, but then none of the families were. There wasn't much in the way of shops, or local amenities such as cinema's or bowling. We had a local butcher, a local grocer, one pub with an off-licence at the side, a church and a primary school that overlooked the river that ran right through the middle of the village. For those kids that were older they had to travel to the next town for high school, with a big red bus picking all the kids up from the same spot in the village – the front of the village green. I'd see them all every morning running down the road, jumpers and bags flailing in the wind, trying their best not to miss the only bus that went to the town that morning. For such a small village we had a surprising number of children living there, which was great for me as I didn't have any siblings, but I knew there would always be someone to play with. Because of the size of the village it also meant there was a lot of space to play outside. That is mostly what I remember about those long, hot summers – playing outside with my friends in the local park, fields and woods… wherever our fancy took us that day. We didn't have mobile phones, so we would knock on each other's doors to ask if anyone wanted to come out and play, which everybody always did, and we would meander around our 'hotspots' until we had collected all of our gang together. Then we would spend endless days creating our own fun. Imagination was a big part of our childhood. We could create fun from anything. Our favourite was to find the tallest trees in our local woods and see how far we could climb, always in the belief that we would eventually reach a magical world that lived above us in the clouds. There were some amazing huge, old trees in those woods. One in particular had an ethereal quality about it, with its thick trunk entwined with the plants and ivy that grew around it, making its appearance both appealing and a little bit creepy. This only added to our determination that there was something magical about that tree, about the whole woods in fact, and so that was where we spent most of our time. In our parallel world there was no reality. There were fairies, pixies, goblins, witches, wizards – you name it, they lived there. One of my particular favourites was a variation on the friendly giant, which happened to be one of my favourite books growing up. He lived right at the top of the tree, in the clouds, which we never quite reached to be able to see him, but in our adolescent minds we had no doubt he lived there and would one day come down to greet us. But in and amongst the long, rustling grass that surrounded our tree we knew we had seen the fairies, pixies and goblins, at least we were sure we had! And, although we'd never actually seen her, we knew that the witch lived inside our tree. Obviously, there was no way anyone could live in a house made of gingerbread, everyone knew that, and anyway – witches weren't all bad, so they don't all want to tempt the children. Some prefer to hide away, living their magical world away from prying eyes. And that's exactly what our local witch did.

As I grew up, I attended the High School in the next town on the big red bus, then to the sixth form attached to it. I wasn't the brightest of children, but I worked hard and I had maintained the vivid imagination that had been the cause of so many adventures as a child. So, once I had finished all the education that was available in the town, I decided I was going to spread my wings and move away to University. I had lived in the small village my entire life, and knew no different, but what I did know was that there was an adventure out there for me. I decided early on that this adventure would need to be a drastic shift from my normal life and would be in the hustle and bustle of a large city, and there was no larger city in the UK than London for me to give myself a culture shock, and a completely new experience. So off I went, one large bag packed, and moved into the dormitories of a London university. My parents weren't happy, of course.

'We're losing our baby girl Gemma!' my mother cried.

'Mammy, you're not losing me!' I soothed, 'London is only an hour and half by train away, you can visit whenever you like.'

Mam sighed, 'But why don't you just get a job in Town like all the others? Go and work for Daddy, you'll need to know the business for when he retires anyway.'

My dad owned a café in the next town. It suited my parents to a tee, Mammy loved baking so every morning she got up early and made Pies, Cakes, Quiches and Sausage Rolls for Dad to sell in the café. She had awful shyness though, she would rarely leave the house, let alone go to work in the shop. So, every morning, whilst the food was still hot from the oven, Dad would pack it up and take it to town. Then he would spend the day serving, chatting and learning all about what was happening from the locals. Then at the end of the day he would return home and regale it all to Mam. She came alive at the mention of any gossip, especially any scandals – of which there were more than you might imagine from such a small place – but still, she would never dare to join dad in the café, and stayed very much a recluse. I never asked her why, but I heard Dad mention it to a few people – 'She just feels awkward trying to make small talk with people, she clams up. No, I couldn't make her come to the town'. It was strange really, as Mam never seemed afraid to talk to people when they knocked at the door, she just seemed afraid to be around them for very long. But I never questioned it, it was just the norm for us.

For University I chose a combination degree of English Literature with History. I loved books. All kinds of books, fantasy, comedy, romance – you name it I would read them. There is something wonderful about taking someone else's words and letting your own imagination turn it in to a type of reality, creating your own characters and worlds based on a skeleton of a description, but adding the texture with your own thoughts and experiences. And then wondering about the next person who will read the book, and what their minds create differently to yours – all from the same words. Yes, books were always going to be a key part of my life, and now study. I'd also long had an affiliation with history, and all things old really. My mind would grow fascinated at anything with a history - a story to be found. The idea that buildings, places, objects had lived for so long, through so much, and could tell us some interesting tales – that they could introduce us to worlds we had no idea about.

Obviously, I carried some guilt for my Mam. She hadn't many friends, or much at all other than Daddy and me, but I knew she'd be fine. During the last couple of years at sixth form I hadn't been around as much as previous anyway. Aside from classes, I had a little part time job working as a waitress in the local restaurant – it wasn't my dream job but it was busy with people coming for country days out, and so the people were nice and the tips were good. I worked there 3 nights a week, and then every Thursday it was student night in the local pub, so myself and the girls would meet for a pizza straight from lessons before indulging in the cheap vodka red bulls and immersing our inner diva's in the ever popular karaoke. Recently I had actually spent an increasing amount of time in the town, so I didn't see much of Mam and Dad, or our house anyway. And once she'd got used to the idea I think Mam was a little bit excited for me – I would get to go and see the world, well London at least, and come back to regale her of all my tales and adventures. Yes, it would be a wonderful thing for us both.

The summer before I left I made sure to spend plenty of time with my friends, we were all moving to different parts of the country to find our dreams and start afresh as adults – away from the childhood memories and people that didn't take us seriously as grownups, and I wanted to soak up every last bit of companionship before it was time to leave. Although we all promised to keep in touch regularly, and visit each other on a rota every other week, I knew it was only a matter of time before that fizzled out and we all became distant memories to each other. That's the thing with growing up and moving on from childhood, you actually do move on. And I was ok with that, if a little scared. I'd never really spent much time outside of my village or local town and so I wasn't used to being in a position where I knew nobody. Plus, I wasn't the most confident of people. You know how some people walk into a room and can just make conversation with anyone, about anything. Well I wasn't one of those people. I would enter a room full of strangers and make awkward, stuttered pleasantries before scanning the room for the buffet / bar / children's table (delete as appropriate) and hide out there for the rest of the period, completely unacknowledged by anyone in the room. But I knew that I would need to push myself out of my comfort zone to make some friends, especially in London if all of my friends were to be believed. Apparently, the people aren't friendly, everyone is in a hurry, and life is one big annoyance to a Londoner. Surely not all Londoners could be like that anyway. Besides, I would be at University so many of the students wouldn't even be from London I wouldn't think. They'll be just like me – I hoped.

3 EXPERIENCES

One of my favourite trees is the blossom tree. I love the delicate little buds, and the beautiful pastel colours – so pretty and ethereal, they brightened up any space and made it feel luxurious and spring-like all year round. So, when I arrived at my university dorms I knew as soon as I looked at it that it was the right place for me - right outside the front door stood a huge, blooming blossom tree in the most delicate whitish pink colour. I am a firm believer in things that are 'meant to be', and I knew the instant that I saw the tree that this was my 'meant to be' sign. I smiled to myself and felt optimistic and ready for my new adventure, breathing in a gulp of fresh air I pushed my way through the communal front door with my head held high and full of self-assurance. Once I stepped inside the dormitory though, it was a different matter. As I dragged my bag up the 2 flights of stairs and in through the communal front door I was shocked by the blandness of the dorm I had been allocated. I suppose all of the dormitories looked like this, they wouldn't want to cater to any particular tastes or expectations, but my gosh they could have at least chosen a different colour to beige! Everything was beige – the walls were a light beige, the carpets were a dark beige and the sofa was a kind of camel beige – that is apart from the black bundle with blonde hair strewn across it. Nonetheless, it wasn't quite enough to dampen my spirits and I carried on down our dormitory corridor, which housed 6 single bedrooms, 2 shared bathrooms and a kitchen / lounge, with a spring in my step and a huge grin on my face, until I arrived into bedroom number 4 – my home for the next 9 months until Summer term ended. My bedroom was as expected, not as beige as the communal areas, but not as clean either. The last inhabitant had clearly covered the walls in posters or stickers of some kind as there was plenty of black, sticky residue left behind. There was a single bed in one corner with a single wardrobe at the end, and a little working desk in the other corner. The bed was stripped completely, as we had to provide our own bedding, and for the first time I wasn't sure that this University thing was for me. I mean, I'd lived at home in a beautifully decorated, well-kept home (Mammy had a lot of time on her hands) and I'd always come back to a smiling face and a warm, home cooked meal. I'd never once had to make my own bed. This was a world away from what I was accustomed to, and I suddenly felt very alone and unsure if I could cope with being thrust into sudden and abrupt adultness. It didn't help that I was actually alone. Mammy had refused to come with me, and although my Dad had offered to drop me and my belongings, I didn't want to cause him any burden as I knew he needed to work, so I'd politely refused and made my own way here on the train. I was bitterly regretting it now – I needed some sort of home comfort, someone to talk to, someone to reassure me and make me feel like this wasn't the scariest thing in the world. Instead I stood in silence, completely unsure what my next move would be. Literally frozen still, I stood for several minutes, frightened to move an inch as if I might go running all the way back home if my legs started to move. So instead, I stood, afraid and alone, not sure what to do with myself.

After what felt like hours, I forced my wobbly legs to move and slowly made my way to the bed and nervously perched on the edge, like I'd been told to sit down in a strangers room and wasn't sure how comfortable I should make myself. My heart was telling my body that I was trespassing in someone else's room, and my brain couldn't overpower my feelings to correct it, and so I felt my limbs go heavy and refuse to move into a comfier position. I sat there for the longest time, unsure on what to do next, and slowly getting cramp in my buttock from hanging on the edge. I needed to do something, but what should I do? Should I unpack? Should I just give up now and go home? I felt heavy nerves in the pit of my stomach, but I wouldn't allow myself to give up now, I couldn't, what would people think after all my bravado about finding a new life. Imagine if I went home after less than thirty minutes here, I'd be a laughingstock. Even I thought I was behaving like a baby, I couldn't imagine what everyone else would think. Besides, I had been certain that this was the right thing for me for so long, and I refused to let my temporary emotions deter me from that. So, I continued to sit in silence, willing my mind to give my body something to do, offer a distraction, but I couldn't find the courage to move. I sat with my mind wandering about what I should do next, until a short time later I heard noises outside and decided to distract myself with what sounded like someone else getting a little tearful – maybe they were scared and alone like me and we could be friends and support each other?! I made my way over to the window and peered out to see a girl leaning against the blossom tree, waving her arms around animatedly as she engaged in conversation with some other newbies. As I watched I realised that the crying was actually laughing. Great, huge belly laughs from the slight girl covered head to toe in dark clothing – and I instantly recognized her as the girl from the sofa, that I'd seen when I entered the dormitory. She was talking animatedly to a couple of boys and the sound of her laugh made my heart lift slightly. It was one of those laughs that was infectious, and I knew in that moment that I needed her as my friend.

Bronagh was her name. And as luck would have it, we did become friends. She was my kindred spirit, my soul mate, my best friend. I'm not sure I would have lasted the first week had I not met Bronagh, she took me under her wing and made me venture outside my room and our dormitory into the Campus outside of our block. Bronagh was the opposite of me, she was full of life and fun and laughter, she had no confidence issues, she was not afraid, and she was unapologetic. She was exactly what I needed. We spent most of the first week in the Student Union bar. Not that I can remember most of it, turns out Freshers week is notorious for cheap drinks and plenty of fun and I got both in ample amounts. I made a herd of new friends and even started to venture outside of the University grounds to some of the cheap and (not so) cheerful bars which ran various student nights throughout the week. I soon found I was actually enjoying University life, and my friendship with Bronagh had brought out a new confidence in me which I liked. During the first few weeks of my new life I stuck to Bronagh like glue, watching her and the way she walked, talked and generally lived life. I found myself imitating some of her ways. I wasn't wanting to change my personality completely, but I loved the way Bronagh held herself in any situation and embraced new experiences. She had an ease about her that I'd never had in unknown places and around new people. I would dare myself at first, to act with more bravery, that was how I developed my newfound confidence. I would walk into a classroom on my own and think what would Bronagh do…. The answer was always the same, she would sit next to someone and introduce herself, without waiting for invitation. So, I pushed myself to do the same. And it worked for me, I made friends everywhere I went. The more I did it, the more I enjoyed the feeling that courage gave me. I was becoming a different person by the day and I liked who I was becoming. I reasoned that this must be why I felt the urge to come on this adventure, I finally trusted in what lay ahead for me here, and that I was heading where I was meant to be. I had come to London with a purpose, a feeling that I could be more, and I felt sure that I was now on the path to find it. I started to live a life I never believed could happen for me, and I loved every minute of it. I was becoming a person that I thought only the most beautiful or wealthy of people could be, intrepid and assured, and I started to believe that I could get myself a life and a career past what had been inherited to me. But as happy as I was, I couldn't shake a nagging feeling deep down that there was something else for me to find in myself, I just wasn't sure when, how or what it was. As the weeks went on strange things started happening to me, and instead of being afraid I felt a calm confidence that this was leading me in the right direction. It started off as small things at first. A robin landing on my windowsill singing to me anytime I was struggling with something, and butterflies regularly fluttering around my head, always providing me with a feeling of peace. But a few weeks in, the strange experiences started to pick up the pace. One evening I was heading to our Student Union alone, it was dark and raining so I had my hood pulled up and I was looking down so the rain didn't make my mascara run, still as I walked I could hear footsteps behind me. The footsteps seemed to get closer and closer to me, and I started to wonder if whoever was there needed to get passed me in a hurry. I hesitated in my walking and turned to see if I needed to move over, only to find there was nobody there. Strange I thought standing still, I definitely heard footsteps, but as I turned to continue my walk a car skidded in the wet and mounted the kerb a few metres in front of me. The exact spot on the kerb that I would have been standing if I hadn't had paused for the footsteps. The footsteps that almost certainly saved my life. I had no idea what was happening, or what I could do to find out more, but I was certain my life still had some growing and learning, and it wouldn't all be down to Bronagh's influence.

4 LOST

As the months went on, I grew familiar with my new surroundings. The first few weeks were a nightmare, I had no idea how to navigate such a large city. I would get lost often, even when I was only on Campus. The Village that I had come from was tiny, possibly not even as large as my new University campus, and I hadn't needed to try very hard to find my way around. The city, however, was a whole different matter. Giant buildings lay one behind the other, each one vying for more sky space. Streets were filling with tube stations and bus stops, which were pretty much identical aside from their names. There were so many new places to learn my way around that I had thought I would never master it. But in time it got easier and whilst I hadn't mastered it as such, I had developed a sense of direction, and my usual haunts became easier to find and recognise. I could almost get to where I was going on autopilot most of the time, and I got lost less and less, but it still happened from time to time and rarely caused me alarm. That was why I didn't think twice on the mid-week evening when I got off the tube and looked around with no recognition. 'I've got no idea where I am!' was the first thought to enter my head as I stepped out of the tube station, and not for the first time that week. This time, however, I felt something was different, and panic immediately rose inside me although I had no idea why I felt such alarm. Bronagh had spent a long-time drilling into me the dangers of the 'dodgy' parts of London, of all cities, so I put my unease down to that, as this place did look very different to what I'd usually see in Central London. Ok, I rationalised with myself, I've just got off the tube, so I knew I was still in London somewhere, but I didn't recognise anything so I must be somewhere I didn't mean to be. As I was still fairly new to the city I was still struggling to match the names of tube stations to the areas in which they resided, but I knew I'd got on at Charing Cross and I'd then counted past the usual 3 stops before my stop – Elephant and Castle, the last stop on the route. But this definitely wasn't where I usually got off. Maybe I'd come out of a different exit – I must have done! 'I'll have to walk!' I told myself, pulling my coat a little tighter and picking up the pace to find my way around the other side of the tube station. Wherever this place is, it is really creepy, I noted. There was none of the usual hustle and bustle you'd expect from the city – even on the outskirts you would see more life than this. And it seemed really dark for the time of day. I'd got on the tube not even 10 minutes before and dusk had hardly started to set. It was 6pm on a June evening, yet here it was in complete darkness. It felt quite cold too, which was strange considering the moderate Summer warmth that had filled the city all day. I looked around as I walked and there was nothing I had passed by before; I was sure of it. 'I really don't think I've got off at the right stop!' I muttered to myself, 'I need to try and ask someone for directions.' I walked on and on looking for a person to help, or a shop that I could call in to for assistance and that's when I noticed, there were no other people around at all. I couldn't ignore the unease any longer and as I strolled along, I became acutely aware that everything surrounding me was very different. The streets were cobbled and showed no lane markings that you would usually expect from the roads. There were also no cars to be seen, which definitely caused alarm bells to ring in my head as that was unheard of for London. There wasn't one inch of London that traffic couldn't be seen or heard, yet this place showed no sight or sound of life. 'What is this place?!' I knew I should turn around and head back to the station I'd just come from. I could just get back on the tube and get off at my actual stop. At the very least I could see what station I'd got off at and give myself some clue as to where I was. But I couldn't bring myself to go back. I was nervous, but also desperate to see what was ahead. There was something in me was telling me to keep going, that there was more to see, and by this point I'd learned to start trusting my inner voices. This place was not normal London, I'm not even sure it was London at all, but it was so much more compelling to keep going – it's like when you've injured yourself and you know you shouldn't keep poking it but you can't help yourself, you just keep doing it regardless. At this point I took a really good look around to get a clear picture of my surroundings when I realised that the only lighting was a few old, Victorian style street Gaslamp's, but they were hard to make out as there was a thick fog in the air. Suddenly something flew overhead and bristled past my ponytail, with the breeze adding to the coolness in the air and causing a chill right down my spine. It looked like a bat, but I couldn't be sure. Whatever it was seemed to be following me. I continued to walk, but then it swooped my head again. Every few minutes I would feel it swoop again, gliding just past my head – not enough to hurt me, but just enough for its presence to be known and for me to grow increasingly wary. I could feel prickles all over my body, like my hairs were standing on end. It was alarming and forced a reminder in me that there was an urgency to turn around and get to a safe place. In the distance I could see a glow, and hope ignited inside me – this must be a house, a pub, some form of life – a safe haven, finally! I continued along my path, picking up my pace, but the light in the distance dimmed and at the same time the streetlamps started to dim. One by one they were disappearing, and the small hum of light was getting less and less. I was aware of a faint noise, that seemed to be getting closer and closer to me, sounding more threatening with each passing second, and just like that the reality of the situation hit me. I was alone, terrified of what was happening and not sure if I could even find my way back. But I immediately wanted to give up and try to find safety, so I turned and ran, salty tears starting to blur my sight, and my legs feeling like they might turn to jelly at any moment. I could hear the strange hissing noise gaining in on me, chasing me, moving closer and closer until I knew I couldn't catch my breath to run much faster. I ran as if my life depended on it, because in that instance I thought it might, then I saw it, in the near distance, the station. As I ran through the station doors everything changed and things became normal again. I was back at the tube station where I had started my journey, as if I hadn't even been anywhere, and the crowds around me were certainly carrying on as normal. I looked out of the exit door and could see the hustle and bustle of a normal London street, nothing like the place I had just run back from.

'What just happened?!' I questioned myself as I took in my surroundings.

Everything seemed normal, and yet I'd got no idea how I'd got here. Did I fall? Bang my head? I started to feel around for something, anything, that might explain this strange sense of confusion. Yes, there it is! A lump! I definitely must have fallen and banged my head. It's so strange though, how did I end up back at the station – did I find my way? Did someone help me? It didn't make any sense at all – I could remember everything so clearly; in fact I was still panting from the run.

But it can't have been real, I can't have just transported back from one station to another. Strange things had been happening to me, but not this level of strange. What I'd just experienced wasn't even strange, it was impossible.

I made my way home in a daze and fumbled for my keys to let myself in my front door, when suddenly the fear and realisation hit me, and I was overcome with emotion. What was happening to me?

'Gemma…. Gem-ma…'

I heard my name in the distance, but I was so engrossed in my apparent lack of reality I wasn't completely sure it wasn't just in my head.

'Oh my god, Gemma are you ok? What happened to you?!'

That sounded real. I turned around, still sobbing and saw Bronagh.

'Aw Jesus, please tell me you're not crying over that boy?! I don't know how many times I need to tell you, he's not worth it…. None of them are. My gran always used to tell me there's plenty more fish in the sea, and there really is. Especially at University. And even more so in London...' Bronagh trailed on, but I couldn't concentrate on what she was saying.

I found myself nodding to Bronagh, agreeing to her assumption that I was crying over a boy. I wasn't ready to start explaining what had happened to me. I couldn't find the words to explain it to myself, let alone another person. I would tell Bronagh at some point, I knew she wouldn't judge me, but I needed to process it in my own head first. I was a very logical person, and I needed to find the logic in this before anyone else became involved. Of all the weird things that had been happening to me, they could all be justified with some sort of reasonable explanation. But this, this was something else. I was afraid now of the intensity the situation was becoming, and I knew I needed to try to find some answers.

After several lectures from Bronagh about the birds, the bees, the boys of this world, she eventually let me settle down in my room with a large glass of Brandy – apparently it relaxes the senses – and forced me to borrow her favourite childhood teddy bear for comfort. Say what you want about Bronagh, but she was a real softy at heart. It definitely didn't fit with her hard exterior, and not many people got to see it, but I saw it regularly. Keeping her childhood teddy 'Doobs' was just one of the many things that exposed her softer side. And tonight, she insisted I keep him, to give me comfort.

'Ah, you know, he has always been there for me,' She explained, 'And he will be there for you. There's nothing so comforting as a Doobs cuddle!' She stated, and I knew she really meant it.

So, I cuddled in to Doobs as Bronagh tucked me in, just like I was a small child, and she slowly turned the light out and left the room. I lay in the darkness, desperately trying to turn my brain off, but thoughts and fears were whizzing through my mind.

'Just go to sleep!' I demanded of myself.

But the more I tried to convince my mind to switch off and go to sleep, the more it seemed to jump in to action.

'Fine!' I sighed, 'I'll get up!'

I knew if I went to the communal kitchen and lounge I would risk disturbing Bronagh, and then I'd have to spend another hour or two discussing the intricate workings of the male mind. So instead I downed my glass of Brandy that was mostly untouched, fired up my laptop and decided to try to find some reasonable answers. Firstly, I checked my emails, and read over an assignment that had been sent through. I was desperately trying to busy myself, in the hope that I would forget to search and find answers to what had happened – maybe I'd become so engrossed in the assignment task that I'd even forget what had happened. I knew I was just delaying – like when you're waiting for the results of a really important exam. You know that when you open the results envelope all of the torture of waiting will be gone, yet you still can't bring yourself to do it – just in case what is inside isn't what you're hoping for and your life is turned upside down in that instance. Ignorance is bliss, at least for those few moments before you uncover the truth, but you know in the end you can't put it off forever and it's best to just rip that plaster right off.

So, I gave in. I decided to sit and search. I was desperately trying to convince myself that nothing strange had happened – of course it hadn't, it was a figment of my imagination. Better yet, a reaction to a tired mind. I'd got off the tube in a scary part of London and in my panic and shock I must have blocked out the memory of getting back to safety. You hear about things like this happening to people all the time, they suffer a trauma and black out forgetting huge parts of their experiences. Some even forget years of their lives. I heard about one woman who awoke from a coma and had no idea who her husband and kids were. I know that's a little extreme for my situation, but I was seriously afraid – and the mind works in mysterious ways, so they say. But just to be sure, I was going to see what I could find on the internet. Just in case anyone else had experienced a similar situation and I could put my mind at rest that I hadn't gone completely mad.

I fired up Google and then I sat there, staring at the blank screen. What could I even search?! I started with 'scary things in London'. I couldn't bring myself to look at first, what if I really had ended up in a gangster part of London and they'd been trying to frighten me away! Mammy had warned me before I came that she'd heard all about these parts of London where the underworld gangsters seemed to live. And Bronagh was always warning me not to go to any part of London I didn't know alone. Would they come looking for me, for trespassing on their 'turf'? Maybe I had interrupted some kind of deal they had going on. Or maybe they were waiting for someone, for a confrontation, and I'd inadvertently got in the way. But my search history showed nothing more than a list of London's Scariest Attractions. Disappointment filled me, but also intrigue. Some of these sounded really quite good… The London Dungeon, Jack The Ripper Tour, The Ghost Bus Tours. I must remember to come back to this page and compile a list of things to do on my days off! I tried another search, this time I went for the tube angle 'strange things at Elephant and Castle Tube Station', but again nothing of any use. Rather amusingly the first thing to pop up was a list of oddities seen on the London Tube, images and all. Everything from someone dressed as half Zebra, complete with 4 legs, to a man sleeping with a parrot on his shoulder, wearing a full eye mask. People really are a different level of strange in cities. Maybe I needed to be more specific. What could I use as my search though? I could hardly write 'got off the tube and was chased by strange hissing noise'! Or could I?! Ah what the heck, I gave it a try. But oddly I found my search mainly pulled up results for problematic toilets! There was the odd ghost story thrown in. Could it be?! I really wasn't sure. I couldn't even talk to anyone about this for fear they'd think I was going mad, but just like that a name popped into my head and I suddenly knew one person that I could talk to about this.

5 BACKSTORY

When I was a very young child my Grandmother lived with us. She was old, and alone, and one day Mammy came back from visiting her and announced she would be moving in. I don't think my Dad was too excited, but he would always do anything to keep Mammy and I happy, so he obligingly did as he was told –moved furniture around and redecorated our rarely used Reception room. To be honest, that was probably a silver lining for my Dad as he always hated that room. It had ended up as a kind of junk room. You know the one, everyone has one, the room where all unused items seem to be moved to, never to see daylight again. God forbid we threw anything away. If we got a new dining set, we'd keep the old one in the 'store' room. If we replaced our hoover, we put the old one away in the 'store' room. We even had my old cot mattress in there, which was clearly never going to be used again. But Mammy insisted, you never know when we might need it, it's always useful to have a spare or two. It was my Dad's worst nightmare, he hated clutter, but he kept quiet to keep the peace. So, when Mammy told him that Grandma would be moving in, he jumped at the opportunity to clear out the clutter and spruce up the room. He did a great job of it too, the new carpet was thick piled and so soft and luxurious, the wallpaper was textured – quite velvety to touch. The room had gone from a 1980's orange and brown monstrosity to a more muted and comforting cream and pale yellow, and I could tell Dad was really proud of his décor skills. Grandma was impressed too. She was overcome with emotion when she saw the room. I was only 6 but I still remember being really frightened of my lovely, sweet nan bursting in to tears at the sight of the room. I understand now that she was probably extremely poignant at the move, she was incredibly independent up until that point and I'm sure moving in with her Daughter, Son-In-Law and Granddaughter was the mark of the end of that independence. But I realise now that she was also very touched by the effort that had gone in to creating her a little space of luxury.

Grandma lived with us for several years, but with each passing year she grew weaker and weaker, and left the house less often. So, I would spend a lot of time with her – playing board games, watching TV, talking about life. Mammy would often join in too and as I grew older, I learnt to ask Grandma as much as I could about life and soak in all she would tell me about her experiences. When I was in year 3 I did a project at school about World War 2 and Grandma was a fountain of knowledge. She insisted Dad retrieve her old, battered, leather suitcase from the loft, and she found out lots of memorabilia from the war for me to take in for show and tell. I was so proud showing off all the different things Grandma had saved. She had a ration book, a gas mask, a letter from my Grandad that he'd sent whilst he was away, a few old newspaper clippings and some of her old uniform – Grandma had been in the Women's Land Army. My teacher was so impressed with what Grandma had taught me, and what she allowed the class to see from her collection, she invited Grandma in to talk to the class about her experiences. At this point Grandma only really left the house once a month, usually to visit the Doctor, but she jumped at the opportunity to talk to the class. And talk she did. It was like she became alive talking about the War. She was enthralling to listen to, and the whole class was engrossed by her – which is a hard thing to achieve in a class of 8- and 9-year olds. Grandma literally lit up the room, and that lit up my heart for her even further. I was so proud of my Grandma, here in my classroom, talking to my friends and peers and filling us all with interesting facts and stories that no teacher could have taught us. Grandma taught the class all about the Women's Land Army, and their importance in the war. She explained how the job was advertised and described as supporting the land so the men could go out and fight, and in return the women involved could go and live in the countryside, working the land and enjoying a healthier and safer lifestyle. It was mainly aimed at city women who were fearful of overnight attacks, and wanted to experience a cleaner, fresher lifestyle. That is how our family ended up living in the countryside, as Grandma didn't want to return to a city after the war ended. She'd originally hailed from London, but after visiting towards the end of the war to see her family, she saw the drastic and devastating effects the war had had on the city and decided to stay in the Cotswolds area which is where we still lived now. My Grandad was one of the lucky ones, he made it out of the war in one piece and carried on to live a full life with Grandma which resulted in them having two children – Mammy and my Uncle Steve. My Uncle Steve was a bit of a rogue, by all accounts, and had moved to Australia when he was 17 as one of the 10-pound Poms. For those that don't know, it was a deal where they could jump on a ferry, with all of their worldly goods, and move to Australia for £10, in a bid to boost residency and the economy. He occasionally called Mammy, but those calls had become increasingly infrequent in recent years and when the calls did come, they were short and sweet. But getting back to Grandma, she filled the class with sweet tales of love and sacrifice, with the odd scary bomb story thrown in for added oohs and aahs, and finished by telling the class how she really believed the war was won on a bit of luck, and a lot of skill with a sprinkling of magic thrown in. I swelled with emotion and delight at the class cheering my Grandma, and I knew at that moment there was nothing more magical than her.

Shortly after Grandma's time in the classroom she started to become increasingly week. Her monthly outings stopped completely, and by the time Christmas rolled around it was the Doctor coming out to visit Grandma, rather than her visiting him. It broke my heart to see my lovely Grandma so frail and vulnerable. One-night Mammy came to talk to me in my room. I thought she was coming to lecture me on the importance of going to bed on Christmas Eve, and being properly asleep so that Santa would come inside with my presents, like she told me every year. But she didn't. She sat on the edge of my bed and held my hand in hers.

'Gemma, listen. I know you are very young to deal with big people situations but, unfortunately, I need you to know about Grandma. Doctor Bronwin came to see her today, and Grandma is very sick.'

'I know Mam, she's been like this for ages. That's why she came to live here.' I replied.

Mammy's eyes filled with tears.

'I know that's why she came to live here sweetheart, but she's getting more and more poorly by the day. It probably won't be long until Grandma is no longer with us.'

'You mean she's going to die, don't you?'

Mammy stayed quiet, her head bowed and her eyes to the

floor.

'I already knew she was getting ready to die Mammy; well I knew they were getting ready to take her.'

Mammy's eyes lifted from the floor and darted to mine, eyebrows raised and quite a horrified look on her face.

'What do you mean, who are going to take her?!' Mammy's voiced sounded urgent and forceful, and I became a little scared.

'Erm, I don't know, I'm not sure. Don't be mad, I just saw them the other day.'

'Saw who Gemma?! What happened? You must tell me! Please don't be scared, I'm not mad, I just need to know what you saw, so I can keep you safe.'

'It was the shadows.'

Mammy's face paled, 'The shadows?'

'They come Mammy, every time something bad happens.'

'Go on…'

'They just come around when bad stuff is going on, and as the time gets close for the bad things, they get closer to me until the bad things happen and then they stop coming, just like that.'

'And they've been coming around again? How do you know it's for Granny?' Mum asked.

'Because I saw them flying last night, and they flew right over the top of her.'

The colour drained from Mammy's face and she started to cry. She held on to me so tightly it hurt just a little, but I didn't say a word, I could sense her fear and I didn't want to upset her more than I already had. I wished I could take back what I'd just told her, obviously the shadows hadn't shown her the bad that was about to happen and now I'd made it more real for her. I was so confused as to how she'd missed the shadows, they seemed to be around almost permanently at the moment, but I daren't ask and upset her anymore.

Less than a week later Granny passed away. It was very peaceful in her sleep, and we were all by her side. Neither Mammy or I mentioned the shadows again, and in time the memory of them became quite faded, until I rarely thought about them at all.

6 MARTHA

Granny's best friend was a buxom woman, with a gentle nature. She was lively, and very loudly spoken, but she had the kindest face, which made you incapable of not smiling when she smiled her broad toothy grin at you, and the warmest eyes that had the power to make you trust her with your deepest darkest secrets. She also had the dirtiest laugh I had ever heard, which along with her grin, was highly infectious. I loved Martha. I never failed to see what Granny had seen in her all those years ago when they'd first became friends. They met as small children, they lived in the same street. Back then they didn't see the importance of education, particularly for the girls, and so granny and Martha had rarely attended school. They preferred to spend their days playing in the streets, and neither set of parents had enforced any kind of structure to their childhood days. Eventually they got sent to work, when they were about 11, and then married before the war began, but they remained thick as thieves through it all. Martha had continued to live in their childhood street following the war, and even though Granny had remained in the country after the war ended, they would visit each other weekly – without fail. They would take it in turns hitch-hiking rides to each other, apart from on the odd occasion when one of them was holed up with some ailment, but their friendship never once faltered. Martha was broken when Granny passed away, more so it seemed than when her beloved husband Bill had passed on a couple of years before. At the time I kind of inherited Martha as my new best friend. As she had been such a large part of our upbringing she had always felt like my second granny, but as time went on we became closer and closer and I considered

Martha to be an important part of my family, and my closest confidante.

Martha lived in the most beautiful part of London, in my opinion, on one of the Mew Streets in South Kensington. If you've never seen them the Mews of London are simply enchanting. It is like another world living within London, where the noise of the traffic dims, and the colours of the flowers pop even brighter against the pastels and pale brickwork of the homes. The streets are cobbled and even the smell of the air is sweeter than the usual aroma of fumes that engulf the city air. Martha had lived here as long as I can remember. I would only ever visit her with Granny, as my parents wouldn't venture into London, but I knew if Mammy had ever visited, she would have loved it. As soon as I turned the corner in to the street, I felt my tension from the previous evening relax slightly. I always felt so safe and happy here, and I'd always longed to have my own house down this very street. But unfortunately, despite their humbler beginnings as stables and servant's accommodation, the Mew Streets of London were now extremely sought after with price tags to demonstrate their popularity. Some were almost as expensive as the mansions that surrounded them. So, they were definitely out of my reach at the moment, but one day I hoped to own one of these stunning homes. Martha's house sat about halfway down the street and was an attractive and inoffensive shade of pale pastel Yellow which she had covered in huge hanging baskets and plant boxes. This was pretty much the norm for the houses down her street, with plants and flowers lining the way, which added to the visionary delight of the street. As I approached, I noticed that Martha had painted her front door and contrasted it to the house with a pale pastel Blue. It made the house look even more beautiful than normal, and my heart filled with love for Martha and her home. I knocked her huge brass door knocker lightly and waited to see if she was home. After a few moments I heard a gentle puff and the door creaked open.

'Gemma my dear, what a pleasure!' Martha exclaimed, her face beaming with delight.

'Ah Martha, the pleasure is all mine!' I said genuinely, returning her smile.

'Come in, come in…' Martha ushered me inside and straight to her sitting room at the back of the house.

I never really understood why she had the living room at the back, as if it were me, I would position mine at the front so I could sit staring at the beautiful street all day. But I suppose being at the back did grant more privacy, as the Mews attracted a lot of visitors – mostly tourists and instagrammers looking for the perfect backdrop.

'I've bought us some homemade scones, and clotted cream from the deli around the corner.' I handed over the paper bag containing the ingredients.

'Well that is perfect as I made some fresh Jam at the weekend. Wait here whilst I pop the kettle on and fetch us some plates.' Martha declared.

I sat down and admired the living room. It hadn't changed much in all the years since I'd started visiting. Her sofa set was a light floral, and her TV was one of the old style boxes with a huge back on it – which I'm sure would have been top of the range in its day, but certainly took up a lot of space in comparison to the thin and wide wonders of today's TV world. I was surprised it still worked, I thought to myself, but Martha made sure to really take care of her belongings and not much got broken in her house. Next to the TV, in the middle of the room stood a huge open fire with a rustic oak beam sitting across the top of it acting as a mantelpiece. It was a gorgeous fireplace, which domineered the room, standing large and proud centre stage. It suited the character of the house to a tee, and it was proudly decorated with photos of family and close friends of Martha. I was perusing them, looking at all of the pictures of my Granny and Grandad, with Martha and Bill, and admiring what a handsome couple both sets were. It gave me a sense of looking into a time machine in order to get a small familiarisation of my Grandad, and the kind of person he was, and it was something I always took my time over whenever I came to Martha's. I recall the memories Granny and Martha had relayed to me time and time again and I admired how happy and carefree they all looked. I longed for their kind of happy – after the war, Granny told me, they all really understood how precious life was, and had such a great appreciation that they were all still well and able to live it, that they made a pact to cherish every moment and enjoy life to the absolute fullest. Even as she'd aged, and became too weak to leave the house, Granny had always found the strength to love and laugh to her fullest. She was tenacious in her ways and was a firm believer in being here for a good time, not a long time.

As I stepped to the side, I noticed that Martha had added a little side table next to her armchair, and had a small glass of water and her glasses propped on top. I assumed this addition was to make it easier to have the necessities within reach and save her getting up and down so much. It was covered by a small doily and looked perfectly in place within her time stood still room.

'Here we go dear.' Martha came in carrying a tray and I became preoccupied from my thought as I busied myself moving her small table to a more central location and clearing it of its contents to allow the tray to take their spot.

Even Martha's tea set was floral – her wedding china, she had once informed me. Martha had come from a moderately wealthy background and obviously a lot of money had been spent on the china as it had lasted 50 years and survived through a war. I picked up the teapot and stirred the teabags around, then left the tea to brew for a few moments longer. Martha divvied up the enormous scones, cream and jam and handed my plate to me.

'So, what do I owe this pleasure young lady?' Martha enquired.

'Ah, you know, I was just passing.' I remarked, whilst trying to avoid Martha's eye. I wasn't a very convincing liar, and Martha picked up on my uncomfortableness and dived on it.

'Really?!' she questioned, 'Because you seem like you've got something on your mind.' The woman was a mind reader!

'Mmmm…' I tried to be non-committal and avoid the subject.

'Come on Duck, you know what they say – a problem shared and all that.'

I wanted to confide in Martha, I knew I could trust her to believe me, but I wasn't really sure what to tell her.

'I think you might think I'm mad.' I told her, but this only piqued her interest further.

'Well then you need to talk to me all the more, we can't have you going around thinking you're mad can we!'

I busied myself pouring the tea, and making up my scone, but I knew that she wouldn't let this go. As kind as Martha was, she was persistent and stubborn. And I didn't really want her to let it go, I knew if anyone wouldn't judge me it would be Martha.

'Something strange happened to me…' I started to explain, still not meeting her eye but I could feel her eyes burning into me. She didn't say a word, leaving a void for me to fill, all the while not moving an inch. I continued.

'I'm not really sure how to explain it. But in a nutshell, I got on the tube last night and when I got off, I was in a really strange place. I mean, I wasn't really paying attention, but I counted down the stops to when I usually get off so I couldn't have been too far away from where I was going but it felt like a different world.'

Martha continued staring at me intently, silently willing me to continue.

'The more I think about it, the more difficulty I have in understanding it. I just thought I was in a scary part of London, but it was more than that. It's hard to explain. But this place just felt otherworldly. I don't know, maybe I'm overreacting.' I sighed.

'What station did you get on at Gemma?' Martha enquired.

'Charing Cross.' I answered, a little bewildered as to the relevance. I could have sworn I swore of flicker of delight cross Martha's face, but before I could place the look she was back to her blank expression and I started to wonder if I'd imagined that too. Maybe I really was going mad.

'Could you please elaborate a little on what exactly you saw whilst you were there,' I looked up at her, and it was her turn to avoid me eye, 'Just so I could get a clearer picture in my OAP mind!' She joked.

So, I continued on with my story and regaled the whole tale, including the strange noise that seemed to chase me and how I had no recollection of getting back to my original tube station once I'd ran through the mysterious tube station doors.

Martha sat for a while, not saying a word, just staring out of her French patio doors in to her small but perfectly set back garden. I wanted to ask her what she was thinking, but I was scared of the answer. Maybe she agreed that I was actually going a bit mad. Maybe I agreed that I was going a bit mad. Tears pricked my eyes, and I felt an urgency to go home. As if she had read my mind again Martha spoke.

'Gemma, I do not think you are mad. In fact, I want to ask you a question, but I need you to think long and hard about the answer. Did you get on the tube at your usual platform?'

I thought for a moment, but Martha continued before I could respond.

'What I mean is, do you know the station well, or could you have got on at the wrong platform, on to the wrong tube?'

My heart sank. She didn't believe me. She thought I'd merely got on at the wrong platform and counted the stations in a different direction. Could that have been what happened, I wondered? Perhaps. It would explain a lot. The more I thought about it the more I conceded that she must be right. There certainly weren't many people at the station. Come to think about it, there were no other people on my tube – that I remember seeing anyway. I must have got on the wrong tube, on a less popular route that took me out to a quieter, more intimidating part of London than most people frequent. I felt slightly ashamed at the fuss I'd made, and again I felt the tears prick my eyes. Within seconds they were falling thick and fast, I couldn't control them, and Martha rushed over and held me tightly to her bosom, hushing me like a small child.

'Gemma, I need you to do something. It's really important.'

I listened, not moving nor making a sound.

'I need you to travel up to Birmingham.'

I looked up at Martha, but again she did not meet my eye.

'I can't explain why,' She went on, 'But you need to go to the library there. Will you do it?'

'Yes.' I replied softly.

'Good.'

I went to speak but Martha continued, stopping me.

'There's a level about halfway up the building that houses some extremely old, and valuable, books. Due to their age, and some of their content, you may struggle in accessing them, but it is important you persist… by any means necessary.'

I looked at Martha and I felt concern about her request.

'Please don't be alarmed Duck!' She smiled gently, 'I really think you will find the answers you need there. Just try not to get caught!' She chuckled gently, trying to lift the mood.

'But what is it I'm looking for?' I questioned.

'Explanations, my dear. I trust you will know when you've found it. Just remember, take what you need. Nothing more, nothing less, and don't remove the book from the library, whatever you do!'

I felt more confused than ever, but as I went to query Martha further, she stood up suddenly and announced she'd got an important engagement to get to. I knew this was a cover because she didn't want to discuss further, but I also knew not to upset her by pushing it further. I would just have to go to Birmingham and have a look at these old books and hope they gave me an answer. But what answer could they offer me? Was it something to do with ghosts, is that what it was? Maybe. Confusion dogged at me, but I felt an urgent need overcome me to go and try to find some answers.

I walked to the front door and thanked Martha for listening, and for not judging, but she merely dismissed the notion she had helped in any way. It was only after we had said our goodbyes and I had rounded the corner back on to the streets of norm in London that I noticed a slip of paper poking out of my pocket. I removed it, unfolded it and stared at the words written in front of me – *What shows you the world, will show you the answers.*

7 BIRMINGHAM

I'd never been to Birmingham before. It was actually not a bad city. In some ways I found I preferred it to London. It was smaller than London, so everything was much closer together and easy to access. Which was good, as they didn't have a tube system to get around easily, and I had no clue about the local buses. I'd decided, after speaking with Martha, that I had to feign illness from my classes the next day and get an early train up to Birmingham. I booked the 7.05am train to Birmingham New Street station and buzzed with anticipation all the way there. During my time in London I had become accustomed to wearing my kitten heels, but today I decided I needed to revert back to the old Gemma. I put on my old faithful trainers and tied them up good and tight. I didn't know what was in store for me, but I knew I needed to be prepared.

As the train slowed and neared the city, I admired the view out of the window. Standing strong in the skyline was an old, traditional church with a huge, great steeple stretching high over the ground. I could instantly tell that it was particularly old and would have seen many changes throughout the city over the years. But it had continued to stand strong, against all of the settings surrounding it, and would always dominate centre stage. It commanded attention, however next to it stood an unusual rounded building, covered in what looked like silver discs. Separately they were eye-catching and beautiful, together they were a force to be reckoned with. I smiled and looked forward to taking a look around this new city.

I headed straight to the library from the train station, which took me about 10 minutes or so to walk to, and again I was struck by the beautiful architecture the city offered, in particular the library. I walked over Centenary square towards the library and took it all in. The building itself was huge, and tiered. It was nothing like the old building I was expecting. Instead it was a modern, striking design of what can only be described as the outlines of circles, upon circles, upon circles. They were a mixture of silver and black and entwined together around all four sides of the squared building. They housed 3 separate blocks of silver and gold, which sat stacked one on top of the other, all above a glass fronted entrance. The top was finished off with a gold cylinder, and I was fascinated as to what this cylinder may hold. I had no idea that the library of Birmingham was such a new building, and I imagined how many feathers would have been ruffled when this futuristic design was unveiled. But there would be no doubting that the design was particularly eye-catching and memorable, and that is clearly what the design was intended for. I was so awestruck by the appearance of the building that I didn't notice the doors were closed and no people were inside as I strolled over awestruck. It was only as I stood yanking the handle that I realised the place was closed.

'You've got to be kidding me!' I tutted.

I looked at the opening hours sign next to the door and saw it didn't open until 11am. What kind of library doesn't open until 11am?! I checked my watch, 9.02 am. So much for getting the early train here to get done and get back. Now I'd have to kill a couple more hours before I could even start to search for what I needed.

'Argh!' I tutted in frustration.

How could I keep myself from going mad for a couple of hours?! Should I just sit here and wait? Maybe that would be the best thing to do, there were some lovely benches opposite which overlooked a pretty cool water feature, so I would sit and watch the children playing and enjoy myself so much that I would lose track of time. I sat down next to a little old lady who was chuckling watching some toddlers playing in the water.

'My Grandchildren.' She told me proudly.

I watched them play. The water feature was a perfect design for this quirky city. It had water jets shooting water up high, however it was only a couple of inches deep, so it was filled with people standing in the middle of it having their picture taking, pretending like they were walking on water. It was clearly a big hit with tourists and children, as it was already filled with people at this early hour. I watched for a while longer and found myself wondering how much time had passed. 9.06am showed on my watch. What?! This can't be right, I've been here for ages, my watch must be broken!

'Excuse me…' I asked the lady next to me, 'You don't have the time, do you?'

She checked her watch.

'It's just after five past nine.' She told me, and immediately went back to watching the children.

This distraction clearly isn't working, I'm going to have to do something to pass the time, I thought. So, I yanked my phone out of my pocket and started searching the app store for a Birmingham walking tour. I'd had one when I moved to

London, and it was great for finding your way around somewhere new and discovering all of the interest places as you go. Instantly several popped up, so I downloaded one and started to search for the best tour. There was a one hour snapshot of the city tour, which I decided would work for me – it would pass an hour and also give me time to stop for breakfast, my stomach was rumbling and I realised, in all of my excitement, I hadn't had so much as a drink, let alone food this morning.

My walking tour took me all over the city. Well, probably not all over, but I saw a lot. I walked around the art gallery, the town hall and council house, before descending down to the canals. Did you know that Birmingham has more miles of canal than Venice?! No, neither did I. But it does, and it's really quite lovely. I walked down to the canal at the side of a hotel and was instantly met with a delightful surprise. The hotel, much like the disc building (which I'd since learned is Selfridges) was very modern. Huge, glass and steel, it looked like something from LA but could not compete with the beauty surrounding it. I passed it by, and walked down the path on to the canal, where I was greeted by scenes from years gone by. The canal basin housed many canal boats, and was surrounded by old buildings, pathways and bridges, which very much reminded me of some of the historic drama's I'd seen from the area. So, this is where it all began, I thought. I walked for miles along the canals, and once I was out of the immediate city centre it was very peaceful. Every so often I saw small café's hidden under huge old buildings, no doubt occupying the basement areas of these offices and restaurants of much larger companies. I would imagine that the canal entrance was probably once the staff entrance, or accommodation, and the intrigue made me decide on one of these for my breakfast. Inside the aptly named Canal Bistro I smiled at the petite-ness of the space. There were 3 bistro type sets of furniture, each housing a small vase with a Sunflower in each, and bright cushions on the seat. It was one of the most inviting places I'd ever been. There was a jolly, rounded man, who reminded me a little of Santa Clause, that served me, and I had a splendid homemade full English, while chatting with Henry – the man who was serving me. Henry was born and bred Birmingham, and gave me the low down on all the local companies, big and small, along with a lot of detail on the history of the buildings and canals. Henry was fascinating, and I found I'd learned more about Birmingham in the hour that I'd been here, than I had in the few months since I'd been in London. I was enjoying the history lesson so much that the time started passing by quickly and it wasn't long before I noticed that it was 10.45am and I could now make my way back to the library and actually get inside.

Once I was inside the library, I was excited by the design and layout, as well as what I might find here. Martha clearly knew what was here for me, but what if I couldn't find it? Would she tell me? I wasn't sure that she would, and I knew I couldn't leave without finding what I needed. I couldn't face being in such a scary situation again, I needed to know what it was and how I could handle it. As I walked through the library, it wasn't hard to find where Martha was directing me to. The escalators ran right through the heart of the library atrium and were surrounded by books, all across the perimeter. It was a wonderful sight, and really quite breathtaking. As I ascended on the escalators, from floor to floor, I noticed that there were a couple of levels where the escalators didn't stop. These floors had hundreds, if not thousands, of old battered books lining the shelves, however access was clearly restricted, and I knew getting to it wouldn't be easy. I needed a solid plan before I attempted to gain access to these restricted areas. If I got caught and thrown out that would just make things harder, so I needed to be cautious. I rode the escalators up and down several times throughout the book Rotunda to get a good look at the area, however I started to gain the attention of a couple of members of staff so I made my way out on to the roof terrace to take some time to think about my best course of action. Like every part of the library, the garden terrace was lovely. It wrapped around the outside of the library and being mid-way up the building it offered a lovely view of the city. I sat on a wooden bench in amongst the plants and felt the warmth of the sun on my face. I loved the sunshiney days of Summer, and today was the first day I'd noticed just how warm the weather was starting to get. For the start of Summer, it was really quite hot, and I basked in the light and heat. I thought about the images, in my mind, of the restricted level and I knew that any kind of attempt to get to it would raise concern. Even just being on it would get people talking. I could imagine there were several regular users of the library who would immediately start to wonder if they could access it, never mind the staff members who would noticc an imposter. I would stand out like a sore thumb, and I couldn't exactly move fast when I didn't know what it was I was looking for, or where I would find it. I pulled out my phone and checked the library's opening times, it would be closing at 5pm so I would just need to bide my time until then.

I busied myself in the library for the remainder of the day. I spent some time reading on the sunny terrace, I took the opportunity to read more about the history of Birmingham and how those magnificent old buildings and spaces had become to be in existence. I visited the Shakespeare room, which was what was housed in the Golden Tower – like a fairy-tale princess, it was well protected and looked after. I even had some late lunch in the café downstairs. I really enjoyed my day, and I wished I could spend longer here. However, I knew that once I ventured out into the main space when the building was locked up the alarm system would be immediately triggered leaving me a small window of time to find what I needed and get out. That was my plan, by the way, I would hide in the toilets shortly before close and wait until the building had been locked up and all of the staff gone before I would rush to the balcony that I needed to be on. It wouldn't be easy, as I wasn't sure exactly how I'd access it, however I guessed I would be able to jump down from the ledge above. Once I was on the level I needed I would speed read through titles on the book spines and find what it was I was looking for. At least, I hoped I could decipher what it was I needed. I felt quietly calm that I would get what I wanted, that familiar feeling of trust from my inner voice, I just had a feeling that it would end well. I was more worried about being caught and arrested afterwards. Firstly I had no idea what I was going to do once I got the information I was looking for, if I tried to leave and the police pulled up and I was hotfooting it with some very old and very valuable books it would look extremely suspicious that I was up to no good. But if I continued to hide within the library no doubt they would scour the building and still find me up to no good. I wasn't sure it was worth the risk, but I knew Martha wouldn't send me in to a dangerous situation without very good reason.

My plan wasn't exactly a glamorous one either. I hadn't factored for smelly toilets. Or for cleaners. Obviously, cleaners were going to come and clean the toilets after hours, I don't know how I couldn't have thought of this. I was certainly no mastermind at this breaking and entering. But I nearly jumped out of my skin when I heard footsteps and conversations shortly after 5.15pm. Initially I wondered if there were other people in the same situation as me. Maybe they'd also got on a strange tube and been recommended to come to the library to find answers. But the familiar smell of bleach soon disturbed me from my thoughts, and I realised the rational explanation was the voices belonged to the cleaners. I was hunched up within the disabled toilet, and I reasoned with myself not to panic. If the worst happened and they found me I'd have to pretend to be knocked out. That could be my excuse for being in the toilet. It wouldn't be ideal, because of course they would phone me an ambulance and I would lose access to the library, but at least I wouldn't get arrested. I needed to try and think of a plan. I heard them cleaning the corridor outside of the toilet block, but how could I move to an area that they had already cleaned and wouldn't be returning to? I racked my brains, but I couldn't think of anything, and they were literally outside the door.

'He's such a horrible boss!' I heard a lady state.

The door was opening, and I could make out through the crack in the corner of the toilet door two ladies stood talking to each. They seem to be engrossed in their conversation and they didn't move, just stood wedged in the doorway chatting to each other.

'Ugh I know, he is such a bully right!' The second lady agreed, 'He's making me work late again today. And he never asks if it's ok, he just expects that I'll do it. Like I haven't got kids and a family to get home to!'

'I know what you're saying. He asked me, but I've got another job to get to after here. He's pretty much told me I'm fired if I don't do it. I just don't know what to do!' The first lady sighed, clearly exasperated.

'Ah sod him, if he fires you, he fires you. Come on, don't get upset.'

Through the crack I could see lady number 2 embrace lady number 1.

'Look, let's grab a quick cuppa and a biccie, we deserve it. Then we can get back to it.'

'I haven't the time.'

'I'll finish up these loos for you when I'm done. I've already done the gents, which we both know are the worst…' They both giggled, and I prayed that they'd go for this cuppa they were talking about.

'No honestly, I need to get done!'

Noooo I shouted in my head.

'Noooo!' Lady number 2 shouted.

Did she hear me?!

'Come on, 5 minutes is all it'll take. Plus, I've got a little pick me up to keep us going.' She flashed a hip flask and with that lady number 2 dragged lady number 1 away.

I waited until they were out of earshot and darted from the ladies to the gent's toilets. I couldn't believe how extremely lucky that was. Well, apart from being stuck in the Men's toilets, which were vaguely cleaner than the Women's but not by much. I perched on a toilet in a stall and waited. I'd heard the cleaners mention that one of them would be working late, so I might have a longer wait than I'd initially hoped for, but at least for now I could rest easy that the first hurdle for me to overcome was well and truly dealt with because there's no way they'd come back in to a room they'd already cleaned when thcy were already so pressed for time.

A couple of hours passed by before I heard someone rattling around outside again, just as a phone ringtone shrilled into life.

'Yeah?' I recognized the voice as lady number 2, 'I'm just finishing up. I've got to whizz through the toilets then I'm done. Meet me outside in 10!' And with that I heard a rumble as she dragged her trolley into the Ladies toilets next door.

True to her word, 8 minutes later she dragged the trolley back out again and down the corridor. I heard some fumbling and a door click, which I guessed was to the cleaning cupboard I'd seen open when I'd switched toilets earlier, and then the footsteps grew fainter and fainter. I waited another 15 minutes, until I could hear nothing at all and then slowly emerged from the toilets and down the corridor into the Rotunda. Everything stood still and deathly quiet, and I knew that I was now alone in the building.

8 SEARCHING

I walked out into the main aspect of the Rotunda and looked up. Everything looked so different at night. There was still plenty of lighting from the city coming through the windows, which allowed me to see everything around me quite clearly. The light from the moon gave everything a wonderful glow, and shadows bounced around the walls. I tentatively took a step forward, and then another one and looked around in wonder. Walls upon walls of books stood before me, and for the first time I felt apprehensive about the job in front of me. How could I hurry to find what I needed when I wasn't even sure what that was?! It's not like I could run to the shelf, get what I needed and run off. I'd just have to browse faster than I'd ever browsed before. I edged towards the escalators, which were by now switched off, and decided I would start at the top and work down. I hiked up the escalators two at a time and when I reached the top level, I hurdled over the first gate and down the few steps that took me to my first restricted level. As I stood and took in the vast quantity of books before me, realisation hit me that no alarm had yet been triggered. This could either mean that either the library had a silent alarm, or the cleaner had forgotten to set it in her haste to leave. I hoped it was the latter, but I couldn't bank on it, so I got to work quickly. I scoured the titles in front of me and I was surprised by some of the books that I found – The Encyclopaedia of Africa, Dinosaurs through the Ages, The Bible… these books were nothing like I imagined them to be, they were quite normal and boring, nothing weird and wonderful that jumped out and signalled their comradery with my experience, and there certainly seemed to be no genre to them. Instead they were a wonderful array of subjects that seemed to only be linked by the colour of their covers. Disappointment engulfed me, but I was determined to find what I needed. I continued to search all of the books, on all of the shelves, and carefully walked around the Rotunda out of sight – so as not to be seen by anyone walking past the huge glassed front of thc building. I couldn't quite reach the books on the top shelves, so after I had searched all of the bottom shelves I proceeded to pull myself on to the railings and lean across on the wall to steady myself as I searched the top shelves. After an hour of searching, and with one of the balconies completely searched I climbed down and sat with my head in my knees. What was I looking for?! I took the slip of paper out of my bag and read it again, *What shows you the world, will show you the answers.* What did that even mean? What was it that showed us the world? Planes maybe? Or maybe it was actually the tube? A book about the tube could explain to me what happened. That's it, I thought, I need to find a book on the history of the tube system. I jumped to my feet and climbed back over the gate and headed to the next restricted access area. I definitely hadn't seen anything about the tube, or any form of travel, in the last section, so the next level must have what I need. Maybe what I needed was a book about hauntings in the tube network, that would certainly explain the strange goings on.

As I wondered back down the escalators, I realised how much time had passed since I'd been out in the main vicinity, and no security guards or police had turned up, and still no alarm had activated. This must mean that the cleaner had forgotten to set the alarm, if there even was one. I breathed a sigh of relief and my mood lightened. As I said before, I was a firm believer in things that are meant to be, and I took this, along with my luck with the cleaners, to be a huge sign that this was meant to be for me. I hopped over the next gate and walked down the few stairs to the last restricted level, and I felt my heart warm – this is it; I could feel it.

I searched and searched the whole of the next level from top to bottom, but I struggled again to find anything of any use. There was certainly nothing to do with any vehicles of any kind, or any supernatural phenomena. I looked around and thought hard. What shows us the world? I must have been thinking about this all wrong. It clearly was nothing to do with any kind of transportation, and so I must need to be looking for something else. I decided to go back over the whole space I'd just looked at and keep more of an open mind – look at it with no preconceptions as to what I was looking for. If I took more time over it then maybe I could consider each book title individually and uncover something that relates to what I'm trying to find. I had lots of time before the library opened so I needed to utilise that and search hard. I looked at my watch, it was just after midnight. I expected to feel tired by this time, but all I felt was a buzz of anticipation. I knew I had to work as hard as I could to find what I needed, it would come to me, I was sure of it. I just needed to think outside of the box! Maybe a book about a box was the thing? Does a box show you the world? It can't be a book about a box. Keep an open mind, I told myself, and I started my search again.

After three more tedious hours of scouring the shelves I'd still found nothing of any use. I'd taken a couple of books off the shelves, just in case they might hold the key – Adventures of an Explorer and Another Planet, Another Life held my greatest hopes, but they produced nothing. I went back over the areas again and again, with each passing hour becoming more frantic. I had to find what I was looking for, I just had to! I'd lost all sense of logic. What did I even need the answers for? I could just forget all about it and move on with my life! But deep down I knew that I couldn't. It would stay burned in my mind forever, and I wouldn't allow myself to stop, not until I had to. Shortly after 6am the sun started to rise, and I felt panic rise in my throat. I knew that in order to open at 11am there must be staff on site before this time and so I needed to hurry. I felt so angry with myself that I thought it would be easy, and now tiredness burned at my eyes and frustration gripped my chest.

'Arrrrgggggghhhh' I screamed.

I hit the steps in front of me and let my anger out.

'WHERE ARE YOU?!' I shouted about nothing and everything.

And that's when I noticed it, a small black book laying on the floor at the edge of the bookcase. I picked it up and stared in disbelief at the title 'Magical Windows'.

9 THE ONE

I stood for what felt like an eternity staring at the words in front of me. A wave of emotion flooded me, and I couldn't place what I felt strongest. Is this even the right thing? I couldn't be sure, but something inside me told me it was. I thought I'd feel excited, but I surprised myself with a part of me that felt nervous. The enormity of the situation hit me. I was trespassing in a public building, and also trespassing in a restricted zone. I didn't really know what the penalty could be, but I was sure it could be serious. Yet as much as I wanted to blame my nerves on the fear of being in trouble, I knew it was because of what I'd just found. I still had a few hours before the library opened, and Martha's words rang in my ears 'Take what you need and put it back!' So, I took the book and sat in a small corner with comfy cushions to read as much as I could. Tiredness started to lag at my eyes, but determination filled my mind. I took a deep breath and opened the first page. There was one solitude line in the middle of the page, bolded 'DO NOT BE AFRAID'. This made me feel afraid. What on earth was I doing?! What am I getting myself in to?! I hesitated but continued to turn to the following page. A map looked back at me from the paper. It was a strange looking map, and I creased my forehead in confusion. It wasn't a sophisticated map; it was nothing like the maps we use to get around today. Instead it looked like the kind of treasure maps we used to draw when we were children, pretending to be Pirates and looking for treasure. A small squiggle ran across the middle of the page and points were starred along it with basic descriptions such as 'DOOR' and 'CONCEALED ENTRANCE'. The title of the page read 'Throop' and I was more confused than before. I turned the next page, hoping for something clearer, maybe some instructions on where I'd been and how I'd got there – an explanation of what I'd experienced would be nice too. However, I was met with another map. This time the title was 'Barton in the Beans', and again there was a kind of treasure map dominating the page. I turned page after page, desperate for some sort of text, something that could help me understand, yet every page had a different treasure map scrawled across it. At the bottom of every page bore the words on the first page 'DO NOT BE AFRAID' and yet they gave no clue to what these maps meant, or where they led to. I continued to flick through the pages and tried to search for clues. As I neared the end of the book, a familiar name jumped out at me - 'Charing Cross Underground' and realisation hit me, the titles were place names. Excitement filled inside me as I studied the map and recognized the station where I'd got on the mysterious tube. I noticed at the top of the stairwell where I should have gone down to my platform stood a starred spot marked 'Entrance no longer in public use, proceed to platform' and next to it stood another set of stairs that stopped much further up than the stairs I usually use. I thought back to the night I got on the tube and remembered thinking to myself that I wasn't as out of breath as I usually would be clambering down the stairs. I thought I must be getting fitter with all of the walking I was doing around London, and up and down the tube staircases, but maybe I just hadn't gone down as many stairs as usual. Maybe I'd gone to this other platform. But where did it take me? The book offered no explanation, and immediately I wanted to go back to find out. I flipped back through some of the pages I had discarded moments earlier and started to recognise other place names that I'd passed over in my haste to find paragraphs of words. 'Brixton' I recognised as one of the London suburbs, 'York Minster' up North, I slowly started to verify the titles as places and I was sure that these places must all have, as the title suggested, Magic Windows.

I glanced again at my watch and knew I didn't have much time to get the information I needed, but I also knew I couldn't take the book with me. I pulled my smartphone out of my pocket and opened up the camera app. I would take pictures of as many of the maps as I could, yet there were hundreds. I'll start with the ones I know, I thought, and slowly scanned the titles for any place names I recognised, prioritising those that were close by to London as these would be the most easily accessible to me. There were a lot that I knew, and I was surprised I'd not noticed all of these places as being different. I suppose they didn't look any different, maybe because they all had concealed entrances. I snapped as many as I could fit in to my phone memory and headed back to the bookcases to slip the book back into place. I could see outside the building was starting to lighten even more slightly and I knew that I only had a few more hours in here. I'd decided to hide back in the toilet until the library had opened and had some visitors, and then I would slip out unnoticed, I hoped. Until then, I thought, I would lay on the cushions and have a small nap. Tiredness dogged at my eyes but once I was out, I knew I would immediately want to head to London and visit one of the places on the map. So, I headed back to the cushioned area, lay down with my coat draped over me and set my alarm for 10am. That way I could be up before anyone came to open up, and safely hidden away in the toilets.

I managed to escape from the library without causing any suspicion. I half expected someone to jump out from behind

CCTV screens and demand to know what I had been up to sneaking into restricted areas and handling classified books, but no one did. I passed out of the doors without a problem and headed for the first train back from London. The journey was slow, much slower than I remembered it being on the way up to Birmingham, and I stared blankly out of the window for most of it. I watched the hills rolling away, one after the other, and imagined what they might be concealing. Did they have 'Magic Windows' hidden within them? Could they lead me to somewhere unknown? What exactly was behind these 'Magic Windows'. Was it something to be afraid of? I desperately wanted my own copy of the library book, so that I could jump off the train right there and then and find the nearest concealed entrance. I searched the internet, but I couldn't find any mention of the book I'd seen, let alone anywhere selling it. It was almost like it didn't exist. I also tried googling some of the places / titles that I'd found in the book, but again nothing special came up. So, I continued to stare out of the window impatiently imagining what lay ahead for me, until we rolled into London Euston.

The station was busy, and it took me a while to navigate myself off the train and outside the front of the building. I'd already found the nearest location to the station and I set off straight there on foot. It felt easier to walk, than battle through the tube stations, and I knew the walk would help me think through my nerves. Did I want to do this? What if I couldn't get back? Would something bad happen to me? But whilst I had reservations, desperation for knowledge burned inside me and I knew I couldn't give up now. I walked for almost half an hour before arriving at Camden Market, which was also enjoying tourist hustle and bustle. I found a seat at one of the street vendors and ordered a hot drink. I needed to get my bearings, as I didn't know this area well, and work out where it was exactly that I needed to go. I sipped on a hot, sweet cup of milky tea and let the warmth fill my throat. I took a deep breath and looked down, studying the map.

'Ha, is that a treasure map?!' A gruff male voiced enquired.

I looked up, aware that I had now become a bit of an amusement to this strange man peering over my shoulder.

'Yes. Yes, it is!' I triumphed back a little bit miffed that he'd spied on my private photo.

'HAHA!' The man bellowed, 'I always loved a bit of a treasure hunt!' He exclaimed with a thick London accent and a broad smile.

'Yes, well good for you. This is a bit of a private hunt.' I told him quite abruptly, willing him to go away.

I turned my back on him in the hope that he would get the message and leave me alone.

'I see,' He continued, 'Well at least you ain't got to go far, Cocka.'

'Excuse me?' I enquired.

'I said you ain't got to go far. Your star there on ya map, it's right on top of the horse.'

'Horse? What Horse?'

'Your one over there, next to the Stables doorway.' The man chuckled and pointed, 'I hope you find what you're looking for…' And with that he winked and walked away.

I looked up in the direction he suggested and saw there were horses surrounding an archway. I walked over and looked around. This is where my 'Magic Window' is? I stood in between two horses and looked at my map again, zooming in to where the star was placed, and sure enough it was located right here on the map. I started to look around carefully, all the time pretending to take pictures like a regular tourist, so I didn't look too obvious and attract attention. I searched all over both of the horses and couldn't find anything that could help me. Maybe I needed to find an inscription or similar, I thought, rather than an entrance, but short of getting on my hands and knees to study the underside of the horses nothing could be found. I huffed and leaned my back against one of the horses whilst staring at the other horse. Maybe if I sit on it, the horse will suddenly come alive and trot me off to another place? Yet, even as I thought it, I knew it sounded ridiculous. Of course, a sculptured horse isn't going to just get up and trot off in the middle of London. I berated myself for thinking wild thoughts and tried to bring it back to some form of reality. There was clearly nothing on the horses that could help me, and to be honest the map looked like it was drawn free hand so it probably couldn't be relied on for complete accuracy. I widened my search a little and started to peruse the floors and the walls, looking for anything which seemed at odds with its surroundings. I proceeded to step inside the doorway of the Horse Tunnel Market and as I rounded the doorway, I saw it, subtle and obscured but definitely there, a small handle tucked behind a bin. A rush of excitement filled the pit of my stomach, I wanted to get in there straight away, but I needed to be careful not to be seen. I stood at the side of the handle, leaning against the wall and lifted my mobile to my ear. I pretended to be having a conversation, to make myself a little less obvious, and continued to observe my surroundings. Things had died down since I first arrived, and those around seemed to be engrossed in conversations. I just needed to wait until I was sure no-one was paying attention and slip inside. But before I knew what was happening, the surface behind me shifted and I fell backwards, inside the wall and to the ground.

10 LEAD ME

It was dark, inside the wall, and gravel dug into my hands as I pushed myself up to a sitting position. It took me a moment to grasp what had just happened and the oddest of thoughts popped into my head, 'It should be darker in here'. I knew there was some light coming from somewhere, because I could see clearly, yet I couldn't see any lights along the walls in front or to the side of me. I felt confused, tired and a little bit dazed, and started to lay myself back down to the ground. I could hear the earth moving against the force of my movements, and another odd thought struck me. 'The pebbles rolling away sound like they are dropping really far down.' I sighed, pushed myself back up to sitting and turned my head to see what was actually behind me. I gasped in horror and recoiled back to the wall I had just emerged through. This couldn't be real, we're in the middle of London I told myself. But I crawled forward again and realised it was. I was sitting on the edge of a concrete projection, overlooking a huge ravine that was hundreds of miles down. The view was breath-taking, if a little terrifying, and I sat for a few moments confused.

'How could this be here, in the middle of a city without anyone knowing?!' I asked myself. But in my heart, I already knew the answer. This was a Magic Window. And what a stunning magic window it was. I sat right on the very brink, legs dangling towards the ground and took a deep breath, filling my lungs with the endless fresh air. The sun was warm against my face and I could see birds flying below me. I could see a River running through the heart of the ravine, and trees dotted along the sides. I felt like I was in between worlds, I was still part of my world, the real world – I had just crossed over that boundary, but I wasn't yet part of this world. I was hidden, in my tiny cave, and I felt a bit like I was encroaching on the privacy of whatever was below, by sitting here and watching them, staying hidden away. I had to get down there and find out what was ahead, but I couldn't see any way down. I stood and held on to the side as I leaned forward slightly, desperate to find a way down, but panic filled me as my footing started to slip. I couldn't risk falling, there was no way I'd make it out alive! I thought back to the book, there must be something in there that could help me. I pulled out the picture on my phone of the map, but that merely showed how to get here, there was nothing I could use to help me get down. I took another deep breath and closed my eyes to concentrate and that's when I saw it in my mind, the page in the book that read DO NOT BE AFRAID.

'Do not be afraid!' I told myself as I opened my eyes.

'That's it.' I continued, 'I am not afraid! I AM NOT AFRAID!' I shouted.

It took me a while to believe what I was saying, but as soon as I did it appeared, like it had always been there. A type of ski lift, right to the side of me, patiently still waiting for someone to climb on to one of the chairs and head down. I stepped on and sat down, curious as to where it would take me. I couldn't see where I was going to end up, yet excitement still rose within me. I was not afraid; I had never felt calmer. I knew that what lay ahead of me now was nothing to be frightened of.

The ride down was like nothing I'd experienced before. It was smooth, beautiful and calming, and I almost didn't want it to come to an end. Yet I jumped off as we reached the base at the ground and walked through a doorway in front of me. The sight that lay ahead of me wasn't what I was expecting. I was expecting to be down in the Valley, perhaps next to a Waterfall that led to the River. Instead I looked out on to a Street, filled with people and houses. At first glance I didn't see anything unusual about the street, but as I stepped out of the door and took a good look around, I realised that this street was a little unusual. For a start nobody even glanced at me, which was quite strange considering I'd just stepped out of a huge, random door in the middle of a residential street. But as I walked, I noticed that the houses were quite out of the ordinary too. On their own they weren't that obvious, however together they looked rather peculiar. The houses along the street were all magnificent, beautiful buildings, yet they were all completely polar worlds apart from each other in terms of appearance. The first house I came to was rather traditional looking. In fact, it looked very much like my cottage at home, except this one was 3 times the size. It had a beautiful thatched roof, with wooden sash windows and thick Ivy covering almost the whole of the front wall of the house. I smiled at the bold, Red front door and instantly thought of Martha – she would definitely approve. I turned and continued walking and looked up at the next house. This house looked more like something from Hollywood. It was the biggest mansion I had ever seen. It was mostly obscured by huge fences and gates, that were then lined by trees almost completely blocking any view. But I could see a large sweeping driveway and an even larger sweeping staircase leading to the pillared front entrance. It was impressive, and I wondered who might live here. I turned to continue my journey but was almost instantly distracted by the house across the street. Now this really was something out of the ordinary. It looked a little bit like the house I imagined the witch had in the story of Hansel and Gretel, you know the one made out of biscuits and sweets, but a little pinker. It actually didn't look real, rather it looked like it belonged in Disneyland, or another one of those kind of theme parks. I couldn't help but admire the craftmanship that must have gone in to creating this building, and a small part of me felt like a child again longing to go inside and see if it was just as crazy. The house itself was like a Bungalow, with the top floor being windows protruding from the roof. All of the windows were rounded at the top, almost like archways, and were paired with wooden shutters either side, decorated with pink and purple hearts. The roof was created using pastel purple, pink and blue slats and again was lined across the top with hollow hearts. The chimney stones were grey and beige, mixed with pale pink, and topped with a bright pink chimney crown standing proud in the air. The little picket fences lining the small pathway up the house were pastel pink, and the front porch of the house was a mixture of bright and pale pink with a pale purple front door. I couldn't decide if I loved or hated the look of this house, but I couldn't take my eyes of it. I realised, I thought it was magnificent. It invoked a real feeling of urgent elation inside me, which was partly because of the house itself taking me right back to childhood, and the feelings I got when reading those fairy tales and truly believing in them and loving the magic of them. But also because of the magic I was experiencing right now and knowing that I'd truly uncovered something special through this Magic Window.

'Ah, you admiring the old house are you?' A man's voice broke through my thoughts.

I turned to see a short, old man stood next to me, also gazing at the house with a look of appreciation in his eyes.

'Erm yes, I am.' I started, 'I've never seen anything quite like it.'

'No, not many people have. That's why I designed her. She's not to everyone's taste mind, but I've had her for almost 30 years now and I still get a feeling of adoration every time I see her.'

We stood in silence for a moment, just staring at the house.

'What was your inspiration?' I asked the old man.

'Magic.' He replied without hesitation.

'Magic.' I repeated.

'I wanted something which truly defined the meaning of magic to me. I wanted something that evoked that innocent and naïve feeling of a magical world we've all felt at one time or another. To me, there's nothing more special than that. Besides, the world is so boring these days, if you can't have fun with magic in the Other World, when can you have fun with it?!' The man giggled.

'Yes.' I agreed, not sure what else to say.

'Would you like a look inside, I'm just about to put on a pot of tea?' The man enquired.

I longed to go in, but I also needed to get to a place where I could understand where I was.

'Erm, I'm not sure I've got time at the moment, but if you don't mind me coming back another time?' I queried.

'Of course you can, anytime!'

And with that the man turned on his heel and wondered into his house. I also turned and continued my walk up the street, and in to the unknown.

11 THE VISITOR CENTRE

I followed the signposts and walked up the road, opposite to where I had come from. I continued to admire the weird and wonderful array of houses that lined the street, as well as enjoying the warmth of the sun on my skin. I felt relaxed and calm, and I realised that I felt genuinely happy. My head was telling me that I shouldn't feel this calm, that I should put up some sort of guarded approach to this unknown world, but my heart felt relaxed and I wanted to enjoy the tranquility it offered. As the road came to an end, I looked out across a busy junction and at a huge great park, that stretched further than the eye could see, with a buzzing main road surrounding it. I crossed over and entered the park through a pair of huge iron gates, which only added to the grandeur of the place. The park itself reminded me a little of Central Park, not that I'd ever been but from pictures I'd seen I guessed it was a little like this. It looked as huge inside as it did outside. There was a winding path that ran throughout, and people were dotted all around on the grass. I joined on to the path, and continued to walk at a relaxed pace, slowly observing everything that was happening around me. There were all kinds of people milling around, also enjoying the sunshine and the lively setting. I sat on a bench to take a break and really observe my surroundings. Over in a shaded corner stood a group of people doing a Yoga class, and I couldn't help but notice how smiley they all looked. I wasn't sure if it was the Yoga, the weather, the wonderful place they were in or a combination of all three, but I wanted to look like them with a smile on my face and relaxation in my body. Maybe I should take up Yoga in the park, I thought, it could be good for my mind as well as my body.

I glanced over to another section of the park that was covered in vibrant, healthy green grass and was bordered by flowers of all varieties. It looked so perfect, like it was man-made rather than natural beauty and I momentarily stilled to observe it. Sat amongst the flower patch were people of all ages. Friends animatedly chatting and catching up on their latest gossip, family enjoying quality time, and couples relaxing together in the midday heat. There were also picnics aplenty, and as I looked at the array of food scattered around the crowds my own stomach started to growl in annoyance. I realised that I hadn't eaten in a while and I was getting really quite hungry, so I decided that I would try and grab a quick bite to eat before I found the Visitor Centre. I got up and walked at a quicker pace through the park until I came across a small hole, in what looked like a rock, complete with a counter and board propped against the wall titled 'Menu'. From afar it looked like there was nothing written on the board, other than the title, so I continued to walk closer until I was stood right in front of it. But still there was nothing written on it. A young girl stood behind the counter was smiling down at her mobile phone, blissfully unaware that a customer had arrived and was stood right in front of her.

'Excuse me.' I whispered.

'Yes,' She answered pleasantly 'What can I get you?' Her accent was strong London, so I knew I wasn't far away from home.

'Erm, I want some food, if you do it?' I asked.

The girl frowned at me, a mixture of confusion and annoyance.

'Er, yeah. Of course, we do. What do you want?' she asked.

'What do you do?' I questioned her back.

'Well, what do you want?' She asked again, slightly more agitated than the first time.

I thought for a moment. The girl looked at me with a slightly puzzled look on her face and I didn't want to make myself too obvious, so I answered her quickly.

'Just a sandwich.' I replied.

'Hmmm?' She was really studying me now.

'Er, a Chicken sandwich, if you do one?'

'Chicken? Just chicken?' She enquired.

'Well, I don't suppose you've got stuffing and gravy too?'

'You're not from around here are you?' She asked me suddenly, eyes narrowing in suspicion.

'I am, I'm just a bit out of sorts.' I lied.

I didn't want her reporting me to someone and me getting removed by security.

'Right…' She didn't look convinced but carried on about her job, 'I'll have your sandwich right with you.'

I turned away, afraid to look at her again in case she questioned me further. I wondered what had made her ask me that. Did I look different to everyone else – maybe I had a different aura? But as I glanced around, I caught sight of the Menu board once again and noticed there was one thing listed underneath the title – Chicken Sandwich with Stuffing and Gravy.

The sandwich was without a doubt the most delicious sandwich I'd ever had. I actually couldn't have made it better if I'd tried, the amount of chicken to gravy was perfectly proportioned, and there was some stuffing but only a very light amount – exactly how I would have made it. I finished it off with a perfect cup of builder's tea and enjoyed the satisfaction of a full tummy. I wanted to sit back and spend some more time enjoying the park and the buzz within it, but my curiosity was getting the better of me at this stage and eagerly I decided to carry on and find the Visitor Centre. There were lots of people around, and I desperately wanted to ask someone for directions, as there were paths coming off at every direction, but I was worried that someone might notice I shouldn't be here and banish me, so I tried to avoid meeting anyone's eye and looked around for something obvious to show me where I needed to go. As luck would have it there was an old-fashioned signpost right in the middle of the crossing paths, and each wooden arrow had a description of what lay down that way. As I perused each one trying to find a description that could help me find the way I needed I felt a pair of eyes watching me and I turned around to find the same girl from the café stood right behind me, eyeing me up.

'Look, it's ok that you're new here. I didn't mean to frighten you.' She exclaimed.

'Ah thanks, but you're wrong, I know where I am. I'm just not from this part.' I lied in panic.

Please don't get me thrown out, I pleaded in my head.

'Where abouts you from then?!' She queried, again eyeing me suspiciously.

'Erm, I'm not sure of the name…' I lied again, 'Just another area.'

I felt my face flush red with embarrassment at the rubbish lies. I'd always been bad at thinking on my feet, but the worry of being asked to leave when I'd come so far just made me panic even more and had resulted in my mind drawing a blank at the unexpected conversation. I looked around for an easy get out, but I felt a light touch on my arm and looked up to see the young girl smiling at me.

'It's ok!' She said softly, 'We've all been… lost'. She smiled again and this time I returned the smile. 'I guess you're looking for the Visitor Centre?' She asked.

'Is that where the lost people go?' I queried with a hopeful shrug.

'Yeah, it is!' She chuckled.

'Well then yes, that's where I'm looking for.' I confirmed.

'Right, well I don't have time to take you there but if you head down that way, cross over the street and continue to walk ahead you'll see some large gates and it's behind there.'

'Thank you,' I told her with complete sincerity, 'I'm Gemma by the way…' I called out to her as she walked away and headed back to her work.

'Everly.' She shouted back to me.

I smiled as I watched her leave, I've just made my first friend here I thought to myself.

I continued to walk through the vast park, picking up the pace a bit. I was starting to feel tired and I wanted to get to the visitor centre while my brain could still concentrate and comprehend what I was about to uncover. I finally reached the far corner of the park and was met with a busy junction. I crossed over and followed a small road sign up a side street, just as Everly had described. The side street was lovely, and it reminded me of a quaint little place I'd stayed on a girlie weekend to the Amalfi coast, all bright blooms and rustic doors. As I walked further away from the park, and what I realised was the centre of this area, the noise quietened, and I revelled in the birds chirping in the background. I rounded a corner and in front of me stood a pair of huge iron gates, covered in plantation, and inside them sat a walkway shielded by ivy that followed a cobbled path beneath it. A small sign stood at the foot of the gate and detailed that I had in fact reached the 'Visitor Centre Entrance'.

I walked along the winding path that ran alongside a sweeping driveway all the way to a grand, old fashioned gothic looking building. As I approached the huge front door, I was struck by the apparent age of it. The double doors that shielded the entrance looked antique and fit in perfectly with the building despite the modern and sleek surroundings found in the rest of the area. The doors were beautifully carved dark wood that depicted various images of what I assumed to be people of significant interest, and had obviously been looked after with real love as they were perfect, despite their obvious age. They reminded me of the type of grand affair you may find at the entrance to a cathedral, and they were certainly a fitting gateway to this prominent building.

As I stepped closer the doors creaked into life, slowly opening to invite me in as I approached. If I hadn't felt certain before, I knew this was my sign that I should be here. I had been invited in, and as I emerged in the entrance hall, I felt confident in what lay ahead despite the nerves trying to work their way back into my mind. I stood still momentarily whilst I surveyed the area and noticed a small desk with a book open on it. Above it a sign read 'Please sign in and await your host', so I did as instructed and proceeded to the table and picked up the aged feather pen that lay in the fold. I dipped the pen in the ink well, and waited for the drips to slow down, but as I did so I looked down and noticed that my details were already completed within the book. Name, Date of Birth, Place of Birth and Time. Confusion dogged at my tired mind for a second as I took in the time on the page. 1.06pm. I looked at the clock on the wall, it read 1.06pm. I double checked my watch, but again it read 1.06pm. Was it always meant to be that I would arrive here on this date, at this time? Or had I filled in my details already, tiredness was playing tricks on my mind? Maybe someone had filled in my details for me? I felt an urgent need to know more, so I completed the only empty space next to my details for my signature and proceeded to wait for my host.

I'd never been very good with demonstrating patience. Even as a small child, I'd get restless and agitated once I decided I wanted something if it wasn't with me immediately. My Dad blamed it on 'Only Child Syndrome', my Mammy told him that was rubbish and all children were like it. I think it was just a personality trait of mine. As I'd grown older my impatience had become less intense than that of a small child with big emotions, but it still reared itself every so often. When I was making plans with friends that I was particularly excited about I would check my phone every 30 seconds until they'd responded. It was like I couldn't concentrate on anything else until I knew the plans were firmly in place. God forbid anyone would need to seek permission and wait for their parents to come home before they could let us know, I literally wouldn't be able to rest, wondering around full of restless energy, trying to find something to distract me for long enough that I would momentarily forget what it was I was waiting for. And I could feel my impatience hitting me full force once more. Sat there, waiting for my host, was the first time I'd really stopped since the tube incident, and I wasn't enjoying it. My mind was racing, and despite my tiredness, my body needed to burn some of my mind's thoughts and energy. Tired body, tired mind. But I knew I couldn't leave, and I wouldn't burn much energy in here. I stood up and wondered around the entrance hall. It was a fairly modest affair. There were 2 doors, one immediately in front as you came in, and one to the left. Over to the right, next to the table and the small stool that sat beside it, lay a large wooden staircase. I tried to peer up it, but I couldn't see very far. The building was typically old in its nature, and as a result was quite dark due to the small windows. I could see the start of a landing at the head of the staircase, but it gave no clues as to what lay in the remainder of the house. It was interesting really, how the entrance hall seemed to be the complete opposite of what you'd expect of such a large looking building from the exterior. I would have assumed that such a large building would have a large entrance hall, not this pokey space. I continued to try and wonder around, but there wasn't much space to move and I sat back down on the stool and instead started to fidget. What if my host isn't actually coming, I thought? I looked at the visitor book and the sign above it, they were covered with dust and I wondered how long it had been since someone had been here.

A long time I guessed. I could look in the book and see the last date someone had signed in before me, I reasoned, and felt quite pleased with myself that I'd come up with a fairly normal suggestion. This was quite out of character for me, usually I'd be coming up with all manner of extravagant plans, like scaling the exterior walls to look in to the windows to see what I could find there – which wouldn't actually be too hard to do with the trestles up the wall, I noted. Still, I decided to go with my initial plan and proceeded to lean over and start to look at the book. The date before mine showed the last person to sign in was only 4 months ago. Ok, maybe not as long as I thought, they must just not be up to date with the cleaning in this place. The person before the last was 7 months ago, and the one before that 8 months ago. So, they have fairly regular visitors, I thought. It seemed strange to think that all of these people have had the same strange experiences and have gone through the same things that I have to be here, and yet more people don't know about this. I wonder if anyone I know has been here, I queried at the same time I started to turn the pages in the visitor book. My mind immediately thought of Granny and Martha. I'm not sure how, but in that moment, I was positive that they'd once been here. That would explain how Martha knew where to direct me. The book was massively thick, and I started to turn the pages in bulk, grabbing handfuls of pages at a time to take me back many years. As I reached the dates between 1939 and 1945, when the war was happening, I slowed and started to peruse the names written down. I reasoned to myself that they wouldn't have been here before then, they'd have been too young, so I'd try searching from here on. My mind filled with a memory of Granny talking about the war, and how a little bit of magic had helped her through it all and a sense of certainty filled me. She had been here, I was meant to be here, this was my path in life and as if on cue a large, old, friendly looking man walked through the door and beamed at me.

'Gemma, sorry!' His gruffly toned voice started, 'I don't usually leave visitors waiting this long, but I got caught up with something briefly. All sorted now though, do you want to come through?'

'Yes.' I responded, slightly mesmerised by this huge, cheerful man who reminded me a little of Santa without the red uniform.

I reached down to collect my bag so that I could follow him and as I did, I again caught a glimpse of the visitor book and there it was, as clear as day – Elsie Jones and Martha Brown, Granny and Martha.

12 GRANNY AND MARTHA

Granny and Martha were a type of magic by themselves. They were a force to be reckoned with, in a very charming way. Even in memories of them, from the depths of my adolescent mind, I recall the way people responded to them. I had always put it down to their absolute penchant for life, and their gratitude for making it through the war. Everywhere they went, they lived in the moment. When they laughed, they laughed hard and everyone around laughed with them. They had an insatiable thirst for fun and joy, and they bounced off each other which only encouraged them more.

As a very small child I vividly remember spending Saturday nights in the local pub. This was back in the day when Mammy still ventured out occasionally, and so once a fortnight we'd head to The Nailers Arms on a Saturday evening, meet Martha and Granny, and eat some dinner and drink some pop. Well, I drank the pop – it was the only time Mammy allowed me to have fizzy drinks - but I guess now that what they were drinking was a lot stronger than what I was given, although they swore to me at the time that it was merely 'Grown Up pop'. It never looked quite as fizzy as mine, nor did mine have as much sugar as theirs did, as I didn't seem to quite get the sugar high they claimed to have. Mammy and Daddy never had too much, well Mammy didn't. Daddy did like to drink a lot faster in the pub than he ever did at home, but we had walked there so I assumed he was just extra thirsty. Martha and Granny were another story. They used to get large bottles of pop to share between the two of them and they rarely ever finished their meals, so that they could save room for more pop. They must have walked really far to be that thirsty, I used to think to myself.

Everyone in the pub knew Granny and Martha. They weren't loud, or disruptive, they were just funny, friendly ladies who took the time to chat to anyone that wanted to chat to them. Their enjoyment of the moment was clearly infectious, judging by the attention they used to receive, and come the time shortly before they stopped going to the pub, they were best friends with the whole village.

As a small child I loved the attention that Granny and Martha generated. Everyone who came over to join us for a chat or a drink would always bring something for me. Mr Connohy, who ran the pub, always came over to check we were ok, and we had enjoyed our meals. When he collected our plates away he would always slip me a small bar of Dairy Milk. Then, over the course of the evening, I'd receive sweets, bubbles, crayons, lollipops, small craft sets and other such items, from various other villagers who would come and join us. Once a month was Karaoke night on a Saturday. It always started quite late, and Mammy and Daddy wouldn't let me stay long as it was passed my bedtime, but they knew how much I loved it so they would always let me stay for a song or two. As a result, this meant that most months Granny and Martha were the first ones up. They'd often let me join them on stage. And they didn't sing old, fashioned soppy songs. No, they were up to date with the latest pop tunes and would belt them out whilst shimmying and shaking all across the stage. I would act as backing dancer, at the front, and pull out my best moves and by the end we'd always have the majority of the pub on their feet dancing along with us.

Those Saturday nights were then, and in some ways still are, the best nights out I've ever had.

Aside from the raucous (well they were for a young child) Saturday nights out, Granny and Martha loved to help people. They spent a lot of their retirement volunteering at local community centres. They would work with Care homes to befriend those that lived there, as well as the relatives, and support in any way they could. If the residents wanted the place decorating, Granny and Martha would enlist the help of the locals that they knew and always get an army of people offering to support, for free of course. When the children's centre needed new equipment to support learning, Granny and Martha were the first ones to offer to assist with fundraising, organising fun days, convincing businesses to donate to the auction and signing friends up for sponsored runs / skydives / abseils. Even Mammy got involved occasionally, spending the best part of a week baking up a storm for a bake sale which ended up raising enough money to buy Christmas presents for an array of families in need.

Granny would also spend her days going around and visiting the elderly who couldn't get out of their homes very often. She would pop in for an hour, usually taking their favourite cake with her, and enjoy a natter over a cup of tea. In the school holidays I'd sometimes join her, it was so much fun. A lot of the people she visited like this didn't get to enjoy much conversation, especially during the week. Typically, they would have families visit them at weekends, if at all, and then they'd spend all week with almost no visitors. So, when Granny would get there, it was always such an enjoyable time, for them and us. I loved hearing all of the old stories from the people we visited, as well as from Granny, and most of them loved hearing my tales of school and what was new in the Village.

When the High School from the Town started to send the bus to collect the older children every day it was like a scandal to some of the older folk we used to coerce with.

'In my day you'd walk!', 'Never would we have expected to get a vehicle!' and 'What are kids today becoming, they don't know they're born!' were amongst the phrases we heard regularly. And this scandal lasted weeks. Well until the local green grocers decided to start selling alcohol too, nearly putting the off licence out of business. The school bus was soon forgotten about then.

I was always fascinated and inspired by Granny and Martha's approach to life. 'Give to others, as you have been given' they'd say. They were firm believers in life having been extremely kind to them, and they wanted to pay it back into the world. It was their ambition for everyone to enjoy life as much as they had, and they worked hard to ensure that as many people as possible had something to enjoy and smile about.

It was the Elsie and Martha magic, people called it, and it certainly was special.

13 WHAT IS THIS PLACE?

As we walked down a dark corridor I wondered where I was being led to. I was expecting rather grand décor inside the visitor centre, judging by the exterior, but I was quietly disappointed by the drab décor.

'Apologies for the surroundings Gemma…' My host started, as if reading my mind, 'We are in the midst of a renovation and so we are having to use the back passages at the moment.'

That's funny, I thought, I don't remember seeing any signs of renovations.

'We try to keep it all hidden, so there are no obvious signs of work being done,' He continued, gosh this man was good, 'So that we have a greater response to the large unveiling when it's all done.'

He turned and smiled at me, 'I trust that it's ok to sit in the garden?'

'Yes.' I nodded, slightly bewildered.

'Perfect, just this way.' He instructed.

As we rounded the corner at the end of the corridor, we entered a large room that was covered in plastic sheeting across the floors and walls – clearly demonstrating the refurbishment that was happening. All across the back side of the room lay huge great glass doors, sat within ceiling height archways and allowing floods of light to enter the room.

'Wow!' I exclaimed, 'That is stunning.'

I was in awe.

'Yes, it's quite something isn't it! We don't utilise this room nearly enough considering its beauty and the stunning backdrop it sits in front of. We'd like to open it up to the community for use, so we are working hard on this space in particular. It will be our masterpiece!'

I stood looking around and taking in all of the glamour and elegance that the room had to offer. The ceiling was high and beautifully crafted in a rounded coffered style. It had clearly had a recent lick of paint, as it was a flawless shade of white, and housed a huge great chandelier in the middle of the room that reflected the light like it was made of diamond. Underneath the plastic beneath my feet I could see pale wooden flooring, which helped the room feel light and airy, and I immediately wished this room was my apartment.

'This way Gemma.'

My host guided me, before I could get too attached to the room, and as I turned to follow him I could see he had opened some patio doors on to a large concrete sweeping set of steps that overlooked a huge grass lawn. I took a step outside and the heat from the sun hit my skin again. I followed my host down the steps and to the right side, where a large marble and iron patio set awaited covered in huge great, colourful cushions. I sat opposite my host and noticed that in front of us both lay glasses as well as china teacups, with the middle of the table being occupied by a jug of iced water and a pot of tea. Just what I would have ordered.

'So, Gemma, you found us!' My host started.

'Yes, I suppose I did.'

'Well done you!' He smiled again, 'I'm sure this is all very strange to you right now, and you probably have a lot of questions, but let's start with some formal introductions. I'm Mr Malahide, but you can call me Malachy.'

'Hi Malachy, I'm Gemma – but you already know that.' And this time it was my turn to smile.

My host chuckled, he really was a very endearing man – I could see why he'd been given this job to greet all the newbies as he had immediately put me at ease with his gentle nature.

'I do indeed know that. So, Gemma, welcome. I know you haven't been here very long, but I do hope everything has been ok for you so far?'

'Yes, it has, thank you. Everyone I've spoken to has been really friendly.'

'Well good, we encourage tolerance and for everyone to be as kind to each other as we can. We've all been in your shoes.'

He hesitated and poured us both a cup of tea and a glass of water. I took a sip from both and leaned back in the seat. I had no idea where I was, or what I was doing here, but I'd never felt so relaxed. I was filled with a strange feeling of familiarity, and I knew that meant that I was where I was meant to be. For a few moments we both sat and watched a couple of Robins on the grass playing what looked like a game of kiss chase. I smiled at them, and let my mind wonder briefly. After a few moments I looked back to my presenter, keen to know more about what was happening to me.

'Right then Gemma…' Malachy's voice broke through my thoughts, 'Let's get to it.'

'Ok.' I responded, not sure what to say at this point.

'Is there anything you want to ask me?'

'Erm, yes, lots of stuff.' I replied.

'Well then, dear girl, please go ahead!'

'My mind is completely blank,' I panicked, my voice quivering, 'I'm not sure what to ask… where to start!'

'Relax, breath, take a moment, and get your thoughts together.'

'Ok,' I breathed deeply and slowed myself down, 'Well firstly, I suppose, I'm just not sure… Erm… Where am I?' I queried.

'Where are you right now, as in here in this building, or where are you in general in this area?' he queried.

'Erm, where this place is generally, I suppose.'

'We are in the Other world.' Malachy started.

He looked at me with a serious expression and I knew not to have any form of distrust in what he was saying.

'Right now, you are in Other England, well Other London to be precise.' Malachy paused.

I wanted to say something to make him continue, but I didn't know what to say. My mind was whirring with intrigue, but also piqued with befuddlement. Luckily Malachy cleared his throat and continued without any further prompting.

'You see, all of the Other world is like the twin version of the world you know, the Real world as we fondly call it. It all began shortly after the hunt and persecution of accused witches, or the witch trials as you may know them, many years ago. Up until that point everyone had practised magic quite freely, it was quite the norm. Everyone has the capability within them, you see. But it's like with anything, some people are better at it than others. Those of privilege and power started to grow frightened of those who worked hard to perfect and strengthen their powers, they started to believe that the magically gifted might start to use their abilities to steal their power, or worse, their fortune. So, a revolt against magic was led by a wealthy and powerful Duke who believed that magic was to be feared, because he himself had never mastered the sense. The Duke convinced people far and wide that magic was dangerous, and those who practised it were evil and out to do them harm. Of course, this created fear and distrust amongst communities and, although many people were familiar with magic, they started to hide its existence within their own family units and treat friends and neighbours with suspicion. Eventually, as the fear grew and took over, it led to mass panic across the globe. Leaders everywhere were advising their people of the imminent dangers of magic, and thus came about the well-known witch trials. It is widely assumed that the Salem Witch Trials were the first, but they are merely the most famous of the so-called witch purge. Magic, actually, is very well regulated and can be a wonderful thing that is used for good. It helps the people and the environment, and a large community were reluctant to give it up. But the genuine people who used magic and wished to live amongst it became frightened, and quite rightly so, that they would be hunted and persecuted. As things started to get really aggressive, a group of the magical elite came together to form an allegiance, known as The Magicus Society, and called upon the most outstanding within the magic world to assist them in protecting their history, beliefs, powers and most of all the people. Between them they devised a shield for their world that can recognise between those with good intentions and those with bad intentions, and ultimately keep out the evil. As a result, it became that they split the cities, towns and villages where they resided, so that those who wished to live within magic could continue to do so safely– just not in the same world they used to live in. Over the many years that have passed since, as The Magicus Society have passed on their abilities to produce and use shields, more and more places have become split between The Real World and The Other World until there is not a place in the whole world now that doesn't have both.'

'Wow, that is incredible Malachy. How awful for those people! So, what happened to the others that chose not to live in the Other world?'

'Well many of them went about their business without any trouble. For many, who had not pursued the art of excelling in magic it was easy for them to hide, and over time it has become a forgotten sense in humans. You see, that is all it really is, another sense – just a complex one, a little like using the brain. It is a shame really, but people are afraid of what they cannot control.'

'And when you say *many* of them went about their business, I assume the ones that didn't became subjected to those barbaric witch trials?'

'Yes, correct. There were few who were stubborn and wanted to continue utilising their magical senses, but also continue to live in a place of familiarity but grave danger – and for those few, many were hunted down and subjected to cruel and torturous trials. Some did not even demonstrate any magical skills but for those who were put on trial it was disregarded how they performed during the trial; the writing was already on the wall – their fate had already been sealed.'

'Oh my gosh, how utterly terrifying!'

'Indeed. And although the world is a lot different these days, the past has left a very bitter taste in the mouths of those who choose to live within magic. Chances are, it could be accepted and widely utilised in this day and age, in the Real World. However, many of the people within our community are just not sure it is worth the risk. They are happy living as they are. Some of them do utilise a small amount of magic in the real world, but for the most part we choose to keep it separate, to protect the safety of us all.'

'That is so interesting Malachy. But I don't understand, how did I come to be here?' I queried.

'Well, Gemma, it is meant to be. You see, those who are keen to experience and utilise their magic, and pursue it, even when they do not know what they are pursuing, will always find their way to the Other world. If it is meant to be, it will be!'

'But how do you know that I have magic in me?'

Malachy chuckled.

'We all still have it inside of us Gemma, a human sense cannot just disappear, it is merely hidden a little in most people. Let me ask you, have you ever had unusual things happen to you?

Do you know, for example, that something bad is coming because of a feeling?'

'Yes – I thought everyone did?'

'Everyone does. But not everyone chooses to trust it. Many people are frightened by the unknown and choose to ignore these signs. Magic is a bit like anything else, the less it's used, the less powerful it becomes. So, for those people that choose to deny the things happening to them are anything other than explainable phenomenon, their magic gets hidden away, buried deep inside. It never goes away completely, but it gets drowned out by the voice of logic that many people choose to follow. I see it more and more, these days, sadly. Since those that understand, learn, practice and live freely within the magic world are now segregated, it means that magic is more hidden in general. Thus, curious people, like yourself, find it harder to access it and become more knowledgeable about it. Although there always have been, and always will be the persistent few who will blindly follow their intuition.'

'So, you're saying that I'm meant to be here, magic for me is meant to be?'

'Just as it was for those before you.'

'You mean like my Granny?!' I questioned and stated in one.

'One of the greats!' Malachy stated, beaming widely with a glint of nostalgia in his eye at the thought.

I was taken by surprise and was desperate to know more, but before I could take a breath Malachy stood up.

'I understand you probably have many more questions

Gemma, but you are very tired, and I must get on now. I suggest you go and get some rest, give yourself time to process your new understanding and come back when your mind is truly ready to learn more.'

Before I could respond Malachy swayed away across the vast lawn. I watched the whole time as he walked away, but before he disappeared from sight Malachy turned back and shouted across, 'One quick rule, you can never tell anyone about the Other world, they have to find it for themselves. Should you tell anyone about it that doesn't already know, you will be blocked from entering the Other World again… Bye for now then!'

And with that, he was gone.

14 AWOKEN

I woke up to banging. My mind was fuzzy, and it took me a minute to come around and realise I was back in my own bed, in my university dorm. The incessant banging was on my door, and I groaned as I shouted, 'Come in.'

Before I even saw who it was, I knew it was Bronagh – is that from experience, or magic I started to wonder as I sat up in bed? My mind filled with memories that I wasn't 100% sure weren't a dream.

'Gemma, where on earth have you been? I've been worried sick!' Bronagh stated, in her usual dramatic fashion.

'Er, I've just been a bit busy, nothing to worry about!' I tried to sound convincing.

'Right, well what exactly have you been busy doing? Because I checked with Susie, Stacey, Becks and Deana and none of them have seen you. I hope you're not still upset over that boy?'

'What boy?' I was puzzled.

'What boy, she says! You know, the one you were breaking your heart about a couple of weeks ago!'

'Ah Bronagh, I was hardly breaking my heart over Ste. We went out a couple of times, I cried one drunken night when I saw him in the pub with someone else, and by the next day I'd forgotten about him. I haven't even given him a second thought!'

And it was true, I hadn't. I'd been much too busy filling my mind with other things.

'Ok, well if not him, what have you been doing?' She pressed on.

I knew she wouldn't let this go. She was like a dog with a bone when she got going.

'It's Martha…' I started, 'She's not been feeling great lately, a little lonely, so I've been spending some time with her.' I lied, instantly feeling awful that I'd brought Martha into this.

Bronagh eyed me with distrust in her eyes, but she didn't push it any further. She knew how much Martha meant to be, especially since my Granny had passed, and she would never question me spending time with her.

'Right…' she continued, a little calmer, 'As long as all is ok. I assume you're still coming tonight?'

'Tonight?' I had no idea what she was talking about.

'Yeah, remember it's Susie's opening night of her show – that Amateur dramatic thing she joined. Look, I don't want to go either but you know she'd be there to support us so we should show our faces.'

'Oh yeah, that. Sure, of course I'll be there…' Although I've got much better things I'd rather be doing, I thought.

'Cool. Well get dressed quick, I'll walk you to your first lecture.'

The day passed by relatively quickly, considering I had so many thoughts occupying my mind. I had gone through a full day of lessons, which only happened to me once a week, and I couldn't recall a single one of them. All I had thought about all day was Malachy, the Other World and Magic. I needed to know more, but I knew that charging back there whilst I was so high on emotion would be like a bull in a china shop. I needed to have some patience, gather my thoughts, and decide what it was I needed to know, and what exactly I would do with that knowledge. I needed to put all thoughts of returning to the Other World out of my mind for tonight, because as soon as I got back to my dormitory I would need to quickly shower, change and be back out of the door if I was to make it to the show in time. And there was no way Bronagh was going to let me out of her sight, without a good excuse, for a long time yet. So, I headed back, quickly changed, and tried to put all thoughts of anything but the play and my friends out of my mind.

'Come on Gemma, HURRY UP!' Bronagh bellowed at me less than 15 minutes after I had got in the door to our dorm.

'Ok, ok, I'm coming!' I shouted back as I swiped on a slick of lipstick.

As much as I loved Bronagh she could be forceful and full on at times. For the most part it had done wonders for me. She was the complete opposite personality to me, and her loud confidence had forced itself upon my quiet timidness and helped me come out of my shell on several occasions. Before Bronagh, I would never have been brave enough to go up to a boy in front of his friends and tell him I liked him. But there I was, a couple of weeks prior, marching up to Ste in front of the whole Uni bar and telling him he looked fit! A little dutch courage helped too, but it was Bronagh that had encouraged me with her words of - 'What's the worst that could happen?'

And right she was, nothing bad did happen. In fact, Ste told me right back that he thought I looked fit too and we spent the rest of the night in the corner of the room barely coming up for air. All be it, that romance didn't last long, but it certainly did wonders for my confidence. I literally don't know how I would have survived London Student life if it hadn't been for Bronagh, but in that instance – hearing her bellow my name for the third time – I wished she'd go away. Seconds later my door swung open...

'Gemma, do you want to come with me, or shall I just leave you to whatever strange things you've been doing?'

This unusual phenomenon of people reading my mind needed to stop. Or maybe I was planting the thoughts in their minds. This could be dangerous territory. I really needed this night out to take my mind off things so I could tackle it more logically with a fresh mind.

'No of course not, look I'm ready!' I waved my ta-da arms to showcase myself.

'Lovely!' Bronagh replied sarcastically, 'Let's go then.'

We walked arm in arm all the way to the small theatre, where we met up with some other friends and acquaintances who had also come to support their various friends and grabbed a drink before settling into our seats.

The night was actually a lot more pleasant than I was expecting, and I did manage to forget about the Other World on odd occasions. The show was unexpectedly hilarious, although the hipflask of vodka we kept sneaking in to our oft drinks probably helped with that, and once it was finished and we met up with Susie, we had already got our names onto the guestlist of a Z-list reality TV celebrities birthday party, curtesy of Bronagh and her ballsy persona. The party was in quite a trendy nightclub and I had a great night chatting to new people and letting my hair down. I even saw a couple of people that I recognised off the TV and I felt a little fizz of excitement that I was in and amongst these types of people. I couldn't wait to tell Mammy, I felt proud of where my life was going, and I wanted to enjoy every moment. I danced, drank free champagne and enjoyed everything the night had to offer. But as the tiredness set in, I found myself wishing I could magic myself back to my bed. And in that moment, I knew, I couldn't relax and enjoy myself until I knew more, much more, about the Other World.

The next morning, I awoke in a panic, willing it to be a decent enough hour to visit Martha. I'd convinced myself, the night prior, that heading to Martha's in the early hours of the morning was not a good idea. Neither was heading to the Other World when I was not familiar with it, and I was already slightly past tipsy. So, I had made my excuses and headed back to the dorms. Luckily my alcohol fuelled state meant that I had gone someway in numbing my frantic state and I had managed to fall asleep for a few hours. I eyed the clock, 11.51am. I jumped out of bed, my goodness I had slept for a lot longer than I'd thought, I was already late for my lectures. I had been hoping to visit Martha early doors and head back in time for my first lecture at 10am, but that plan was definitely not running to course. I leapt out of my room and headed for the bathroom for a quick shower when I saw Bronagh casually sitting in the living room.

'Oh Hey,' She called, 'What happened to you last night?'

'Er, I was sick – too much to drink!' I lied.

'Yeah, well you do look rough!' She chuckled, 'It was great to have you back out with us though – I've missed you!'

My heart lurched a little, I felt uncomfortable lying so much to Bronagh, and I definitely felt uncomfortable wishing her away.

'I missed you too!' I smiled sincerely, 'But why aren't you at lectures?'

'Uh, I'm sick too! Wanna watch old movies and eat junk food with me?'

'I can't.' I shrugged.

'Why not?' Bronagh eyed me suspiciously.

'I've already missed some of my lectures, I can't afford to miss anymore. I don't want to fall behind!' The lies tumbled from my mouth again.

'Oh, you're right I suppose. My sensible voice of reason, as always! I don't want to fall behind either. I'll come to the next lecture with you!'

Nooooo I silently screamed, but Bronagh insisted and try as I might, I couldn't shake her all day. By the time early evening rolled around Bronagh was starting to wilt and I silently pleaded she would give up on me. As she announced she was getting some rest that evening I quickly seized my opportunity and told her I needed to head in to town to get a present for my Mammy – it was her birthday soon, I explained, and I needed to get something to post to her in case I couldn't make it back. I'd forgotten all about it, I told her. Bronagh said she couldn't think of anything worse to be doing at that moment in time, just as I guessed she would, and so left me to wander off alone – finally! I raced to the tube station, and across London and arrived outside Martha's door just after 6pm. As I stood outside it, I wondered what I was going to say. Or what she would say to me. Did I want to know more? It could irrevocably change my life, and I was quite happy with the way things were. But life had already been changed and I knew there was no going back. There was no unforgetting what I'd already learnt, and so I lifted my hand to knock on the door. As I slowly raised my arm, ready to bang hard, the door promptly swung open in front of me.

'Oh!' I exclaimed in surprise.

'Come on in Gemma.' I heard Martha shout.

I wondered into the hallway and shut the door behind me. Was that magic? Did the door just open by itself, or was my hangover sending me delusional? Or had Martha always been able to do things like had? How had I not noticed before?

'Come on Gemma, ask me your questions rather than standing in the hallway wondering to yourself.'

Huh? I strolled in and sat next to Martha's chair, just as she was pouring a freshly brewed pot of tea.

'Hi.' I started; I wasn't sure what else to say.

'Hi.' She smiled warmly at me, leaving an opportunity for me to speak more.

I took the cup of tea and let the warmth radiate through my hands as I held it. I wasn't very good with surprises, and big situations, I always seemed to get a shiver in me when I was a bit stressed. Even though it was warm outside, my hands were cold from the anxiousness within me, I realised, and the tea was a welcome relief from that. I took a big gulp and then looked up to Martha, but I couldn't find any words to speak.

'It's ok, my dear,' She began, 'We've all been in your shoes. Those of us who know anyway. I understand your head is spinning with questions, and you're unsure of everything around you at the moment. But it will settle down. Of course, you will have questions always, this is a journey that you will never stop learning on, but your desire to instantly know everything will ease off. So, let's relax and take it one step at a time, and don't put too much pressure on yourself to know everything all at once.'

I smiled at Martha, she was such a kind lady and always knew the right thing to say.

'How did you find out?' I queried.

'Much the same as you really my dear. I'd always known there was something a little different in me, I would know if something was a good idea or not. As I got older, I started to rely on these feelings and test them. I pretended to my friends that I was clairvoyant, little did I know that in a roundabout way I kind of was. So, I would encourage them to ask me if they should do things like get a certain job, date a certain person, and if I truly relied on my intuition I was usually correct. The more I utilised my intuition, the stronger it became, until I started having premonitions that I found a little bit unsettling. I didn't know what was happening, or how I could control it, and I was fearful of it. Luckily by this point in my life I was as thick as thieves with your Granny, and one night I mentioned it to her. Much like I did with you, she directed me to seek answers and told me to go and talk to an old willow tree in the woods, things were a little harder to find back then you see. Ha, I thought she was absolutely raving mad, but I could tell she was deadly serious about it. And I trusted that woman with my life, so the next day off I went. It was a warm day, a bit like today, and I took myself a little picnic and sat at the tree talking for the best part of an hour. It felt great to get everything off my chest, and every so often a little bird in the tree would tweet back to me like he was responding. I thought your Granny had sent me there for a bit of tree therapy, ha ha, like talking to the tree would make it all better. But as I got up to go, the bird starting tweeting like crazy at me from a branch just above me. Each time I tried to walk away it would swoop down and fly right in front of my face and back up to its branch. It was like it was showing me something. So, I followed it up. But every time I reached the branch it had tweeted from it would fly up to the next one. I have never been an active person, and climbing trees was my worst nightmare, but I was compelled to keep following this strange little bird all the way to the top until I saw a handle attached to the tip of the trunk. Curiosity has always got the better of me, so I reached out for it. As it opened, I could see little that was beyond it, as I was almost blinded by bright light. But something inside me told me to continue, and so I did, along with the bird. The same bird continued tweeting at me from inside the door, so I followed him all the way to the Visitor Centre.'

'Wow, so you grew up with no idea too?!'

'Not many people do know when they are growing up Gemma. It is unusual for a small child to be born and spend its life within the other world. Both parents have to know about it, and want for their child to be raised there, but most people are frightened that the child could never adjust to the Real World if they have only ever known the Other World. So, it is the norm for parents to raise their children in the Real World and either visit the Other World frequently or trust that if they were meant to know about the Other World they will when the time is right.'

'So, what about my Granny, how did she know?'

'Ah well, your Granny was very special Gemma. She had magic thick within her blood. Both her parents practised magic, and so she found out from quite an early age that there was an Other World. She recalls being at home with her parents and just hearing a voice in her head advising her to ask about the Other World. So, she did, and as she did so a kind of vortex appeared in their back garden. Her parents advised her to go and see for herself, so, with them right behind her, she walked straight into the vortex.'

'Oh my gosh, wasn't she afraid?'

'She wasn't really old enough to understand the enormity of it, and her parents were with her, so no – I don't think she was. She was only about 9 or 10, from what I remember, and it became the norm for your Granny to live between the two worlds. She had friends on both sides, but I was her first friend who lived between the two, like she did, and that cemented our lifelong friendship. I learned so much from your

Granny, Gemma, I do miss her terribly.'

'I do too. I wish she were here to answer my questions. Maybe take me to the Other World and help me learn all about it.'

'Gemma, your Granny will always be with you, guiding you. Her body may no longer be here, but her magic will always live on in you. You are merely a continuation of your ancestors. They stay alive within you. If you ask her a question, she will always find a way of getting the answer to you, from deep within.'

I sat for a while, tears prickling at my eyes with the thought that Granny might still be able to communicate with me in some way. I missed her desperately, and this lifeline that part of her was still available to me made me want to do nothing else but speak to her.

'Gemma, I know you've only been the once and will probably want to do your own exploring, but if you want to I would love to show you our special place in the Other World, mine and your Granny's I mean? Whenever you're ready.'

I looked up.

'Yes, I would love that… In fact, I'm ready right now.'

15 SEEING THINGS DIFFERENTLY

'All of the people on these Mews live in both worlds Gemma.' Martha explained to me as we walked to the dead end of her street.

'Oh really?'

'Yes, that's part of the reason they have become so expensive you see. This street in particular, but a couple of the other Mews too, have their own access to the Other World. So, they are extremely sought after for those who live with magic, as they can easily flit between the two worlds. Obviously, since they have gained in popularity, we have to be more careful there's no tourists around – the last thing we'd want is for one of our hidden entrances showing up on that Pinsta thing!'

I laughed.

'It's Instagram, I think you mean.'

'Ah whatever that thing wants to be called. I don't really get Social Media. Too much trouble, nothing wrong with a bit of privacy in life. But what do I know!' Martha winked at me.

We approached the end of the street and came to an old-style rock wall, which was where they had built against the end of an excavated hillside. Martha turned and walked to the edge of the wall that led us almost to the last house, but just in between lay a small gap.

'I have never noticed that before!' I remarked, slightly surprised as I thought I knew these streets so well.

'No, nobody does Gemma. Why would you? Even if you did you would just assume it led to Enid's house.'

I walked alongside Martha, feeling a little nervous, and we rounded the wall to the other side. No bright lights, or borders, but I knew instantly we had crossed into the Other World. It had a wonderful feeling and atmosphere, and quickly made me smile. It looked like we were on just another London street, but this one was cleaner, and quieter and seemed a little bit brighter.

'Right then, this way. Not far to go!' Martha explained.

We walked down the street, which was very similar to Martha's Mew Street.

'It looks so normal!' I exclaimed.

'It is Gemma. Obviously, a bit of magic helps keep things in tip top condition, but we all use our magic to keep our houses in tip top condition in the Real World. It's just that my street is full of magic, so all the houses look as perfect as can be in comparison to other streets.'

It made perfect sense when I thought about it. That certainly explained the appeal to some of the Mew Streets, and why they were so instagrammable. They were filled with magic, as well as love.

'But the first street I walked down was filled with these crazy, huge houses?' I queried.

'Mmmm, yes. Well Gemma, as I explained before, the Other World lives fairly parallel to the Real World. Therefore, there are some ego's that like things large and in your face. They just have a little bit more capability here to build them. You must have been in Little Hollywood?' She questioned.

'I've no idea.'

'Was there a large park at the end of the street?'

'Yes! It was fabulous! Then the Visitor Centre was over the other side of the park and across the street.'

'Ah – I forgot to mention that bit Gemma. The Visitor Centre actually moves. It is the only building that does, but we enabled it to move so that it was always close by when a new person arrives!'

I frowned, a little puzzled.

'But the girl in the park knew where it was?' I queried, 'She pointed it out to me.'

'Yes, she would have. There are only so many entrances to the Other World, and so there are only so many places a new person can get in, you see. There are set places for the Visitor Centre to move to. As soon as she realised you were new, she would have known where the Visitor Centre would be.'

'That is amazing,' I stated genuinely, 'But why don't they have it just inside the entrances?'

'Ah now, we wouldn't want to make it too easy would we!' Martha giggled, and I smiled at her cheeky sense of humour.

We continued to walk and just as I started to wonder about where we were going Martha stopped, and gestured behind me.

'Here we are!' She gestured.

I turned around and saw a side street that was alive with lights, music and chatter. It was an amazing sight and excitement rushed through me. We stood for a while, and I took in everything that stood before me. I could see that there were several small coves into the buildings, which were a mixture of little bars and food counters. Overhead were thin arches of lights, of all different colours, lighting the street like a rainbow – intertwined with string lights to add to the effect. The walls were covered with plants and beautiful flowers, which popped with colour thanks to the lights shining bright on them. There were small bistro tables spread all around the pedestrian street, and they were heaving with people out enjoying the Summer evening. The street was filled with Latino style music that was up-tempo and loud enough to enjoy but not loud enough to ruin your conversation. The whole place was buzzing and I had already fallen in love.

'This place, down here, was our favourite Gemma.' And I quickly followed Martha to where she was showing me.

We walked up the street and took time to look around at everything we passed by, taking in all of the sights and atmosphere. This place was truly amazing, like something you would see in a film based in an exotic location, not the centre of London. We walked about two thirds of the way down the street and then an older man jumped out on us.

'Martha!' He exclaimed in a thick French accent, 'You not been here in so long. We miss you!' He announced, kissing both of Martha's cheeks in turn.

'I'm so sorry Gabriel. I'm getting old now, and not out as often as I used to be!'

They both chuckled, and I could tell they were good friends.

'And who is this lovely lady?' Gabriel turned his attention to me.

But no quicker had he looked at me, he face shadowed with surprise.

'Jane?' He queried, looking puzzled.

It was my turn to look puzzled.

'Huh?' I questioned.

'No, no!' Martha interrupted, 'This is Gemma – Elsie's granddaughter. It's her first proper time here!'

Gabriel's face lifted as he understood the situation and he gestured towards a table for us.

'Ah, welcome, welcome! Pleasure to meet you Gemma, please sit down and enjoy!'

We sat down and Martha ordered us some tea and some pastries.

'They are to die for here Gemma, literally the best I've ever had!' Martha declared.

'Ooh great,' I responded, 'But Martha, how did that man know my Mother's name?'

Confusion took over my face, I could feel it.

'Well because he's met your Mother, Gemma,' Martha gently explained, 'She's been here with your Granny and I many times.'

'You mean, Mammy knows about the Other world too?' Shock filled me.

'Yes dear. She does.'

'And Daddy?'

'No. Your Daddy doesn't know. That's why your Mammy hasn't encouraged things more with you. She wasn't sure if you were meant for the Other world or not.'

'So, if Daddy doesn't know, I'm guessing Mammy doesn't come to the Other World often?'

'Yes Gemma, you're correct. She gave it up for your Daddy. It's quite common. It is a bit of a shame for your Mam, as she was so good at magic, and so loved the Other world. Part of her is terrified of someone finding out about her in the Real world, she would have loved to have lived full time in the Other world and act freely. But she loved your Daddy more than magic, so she committed to the Real world, and a life with little magic for him. Lovely pair they are though!'

'Oh, my goodness, is that why Mammy is so hesitant to leave the house?' Realisation dawned on me.

'Yes, I'm afraid it is. One day she almost got caught out by one of the neighbours, when she was working in the café. There had been an incident in the Town – a little boy had been knocked off his bike, and the whole café was talking about it. Your Mam, without thinking, started to tell everyone that it would end up ok, her feelings were telling her that it wasn't as serious as it first seemed. Of course, she was just trying to reassure everyone, but people wanted to know what she meant, how she knew. After that, she was afraid of exposing herself, so she went out very little.'

'Poor Mammy! What did my Dad say about her not wanting to go out anymore?'

'Well your Dad loves your Mam very much – he would do anything for her, and you, so he never questioned it when she said she didn't want to go out anymore. At first, she just told him she was unwell, then she wasn't up for it, and over time he stopped asking and just accepted that she no longer wanted to work in the café or leave the house very often.'

'That is so sad!' My heart dropped a little for Mammy, 'I can't believe she's lived this lie her whole life.'

'That's the price you pay sometimes Gemma, the Other World and Magic is a wonderful thing, but it can be a little hard to manage at times. Especially when you're trying to co-exist in the Real World.'

Just then Gabriel came over with our Tea and Pastries. Martha had ordered us a Croissant each, and they were huge. On the side of the plate were tiny pots of jam, and I wrenched mine open and smeared it on. The croissants were still warm, and the jam melted into them making a sticky but ridiculously delicious mess. Gabriel sat down with us, clutching a hot coffee and the aroma from the fresh coffee and the fresh croissants filled my nose.

'Gabriel, I could literally live here smelling these smells and eating this amazing food.' I told him.

'Haha, Gemma.' His pronunciation of my name almost made it sound like Shemma, and I liked it, 'You are too kind!'

'I knew you'd love it here!' Martha told me.

'It is honestly the most fabulous place I have ever been to!' I admitted.

'Yes, it is fabulous,' Gabriel joined in, 'I have lived and worked here for many years, and I never get tired of it.'

'All down the street are different food and drink places Gemma, so it is a great place to come with friends as there is so much choice.' Martha explained.

'Obviously mine is the best…' Gabriel winked, 'But these days there are all kinds of up and coming foods and drink.'

'Ooh, and I am starving!' I admitted.

'Have a wonder Gemma, I'll wait right here for you.' Martha directed me.

'Do either of you want anything?' I enquired, as I pushed myself up.

'No, thank you.' They both said in time, and so I wondered off down the street.

Gabriel was right, there were some amazing things on offer down the street. Japanese, Thai, Burgers – you name it, it was there. I was drawn to a sign that was advertising Buddha bowls and headed over.

'Hi there.' a young hipster type greeted me.

'Hi.' I smiled, 'Er, what do you do on your Buddha bowls?' I queried.

'What do you want?' He winked.

'Ah, yes, I've done this before!' I laughed and the hipster laughed too.

'You're new, are you?' The familiar questioned popped up again.

'Yes. It's my second time. Well, my third time technically, but my second good experience!' I stated.

'Ah, they tried to keep you out the first time then?' He winked again.

'That must have been it!' I chuckled.

'Right, so you can tell me what you want – or you can leave me to guess and see how well I can read you?' He flirted a little.

'Go on then!' I flirted right back, 'Give it your best shot!'

He turned and started to get to work on my Buddha bowl and I noticed his muscles peeking out from underneath his short sleeves. Mmm, I thought, charming and fit – they make them a bit cuter around here. He turned back around just in time to catch me checking out his bum. I laughed and blushed. He blushed too. I could feel him starting to quieten up, and realised he seemed a little bit shy now, nervous even.

'So…' he started, 'If you could choose right now – what would you put in your bowl?'

He hid the ready-made bowl so I couldn't see what he had

actually put in it.

'Erm, well I would start with some brown rice.'

'Yep.' He nodded.

'And some spinach and sweet potatoes…'

'Mmm Hmmm.'

'Topped with some chickpeas and thinly sliced carrot and cucumber.'

'How about some crushed nuts?'

'Ooh yes, perfect! With some sort of dressing – tangy, not too sweet?'

'Ginger and Garlic Soy perhaps?'

'Oh my gosh, yes! Sounds amazing!'

He slid the bowl across the counter to me and smiled.

'Nooo, you didn't!' I was impressed, 'Thank you!'

'No problem at all….Erm…?'

'Gemma.' I told him.

I don't know how; I just knew he was trying for my name. And I was happy to give it to him.

'No problem at all, Gemma!' His eyes darted to the floor, and I could feel his shyness reappearing.

'How much do I owe you, Erm…?'

'Nicholas.' He told me, 'And nothing, it's on me.'

'Ah thank you, but I can't!' I argued.

'No, no. I insist. As a welcome gift.'

'Thank you very much Nicholas.' I smiled.

'No problem, I hope to see you again soon.'

He blushed again.

'You definitely will!' I told him as I turned to walk away.

I loved this place already.

The rest of the night flew by much too quickly. I talked and laughed, and drank a few cocktails with Martha and Gabriel, and I realised at the end of the evening that I'd had one of the best nights I'd had in a long time. The atmosphere, the music, the setting was all so perfect, and I could see why Granny and Martha had deemed it their favourite place. It was shortly after 10.30pm when Martha announced that she was too long in the tooth to be out all night, her words, and she needed to be getting back to her knitting. I chuckled and stood to walk with her.

'I do hope you will be back Gemma, that we have shown you a good time?' Gabriel enquired.

'Ah yes, definitely. I've loved every minute of it!' I exclaimed.

And I meant it. I knew that I couldn't be one of those people that chose not to live amongst magic, and the Other world. The more I experienced it, the more I wanted of it. Most of all, I knew it wouldn't be long until I was back again.

'Good! Live amongst it, learn, and enjoy!' He spoke softly and warmly.

'I will, thank you!'

'And don't worry about Nicholas, Martha gave me your number to give to him later.' He stated with a gleam in his eye, and a giggle in his voice.

I blushed hard, and wondered how they knew, but I asked no questions and made no protests.

16 BACK IN THE REAL WORLD

I decided that I would try to live in normality for a few days. Well, what normality had been for me before the last crazy couple of weeks. I was falling behind on my University work, which was not something I wanted to do. I wasn't sure if I would use my degree, or even live in the Real world at all, but I knew that I needed to give myself some options especially with the Other World being so new and unknown to me. I buckled down and caught up on the work that I'd missed and made sure to attend every lecture as I had before. I was reliable and hardworking, usually, so the last couple of weeks had been completely out of character for me, and it hadn't gone unnoticed. Obviously Bronagh had picked up on it, but so had most of my other friends, as well as some of my lecturers. All week I had people asking me if everything was ok, if I needed any support with anything. I felt terrible lying to those who clearly cared for me, but I had lied to cover my erratic actions and so I told everyone that I was becoming overwhelmed with the workload. To some degree, I was. But only because I'd fallen behind. I felt so guilty lying further, and causing so much concern for me, especially when I was secretly having the best time of my life. I also felt guilty for Mammy. I really needed to speak with her and let her know that I knew. I knew all about her magic, about her past, and I wanted to tell her that she was finally free to be herself with me. I had checked with Martha and she had said it was fine to tell the people who already knew about magic what I had uncovered. But I decided that it would require a trip back home and a face to face conversation, and I just couldn't lose any more time at the moment. So, I stayed at Uni, and worked hard to bring myself back up to speed. It was heart-warming to see my friends and teachers trying so hard to assist me and I started to wonder if I really did want to leave the Real World. I had so many good friends and family around me, could I really leave them all behind? It was certainly a question that I would put some careful thought in to, but for now I would enjoy everything the Real world had to offer me and try to continue to learn about the Other World where I could.

At the same time as catching back up on my University work, I also spent a little time alone to practise some of my magic. I had a lot of time on my own, sat at my laptop, and every so often I would take a little break and do a kind of meditation to focus on my inner voice. This is what Martha had told me to do to build my intuition, and magic sense. The more you listen to it, the stronger it will become. It was difficult at first, I wasn't sure whether I was forcing myself to feel things that weren't there, just because I wanted it so much. But a few nights in, I felt an overwhelming sense that my University work would be good, and I believed it.

A week after I had been to the Other World with Martha, I was just finishing up a particularly gruelling assignment and feeling quite pleased with myself for working so hard to get it done, when I heard a familiar vibrate from my phone. I assumed it was Bronagh and decided that wherever she was inviting me to I would go. I needed a little break before starting anything else and a small drink wouldn't hurt to get my creative juices flowing.

HI GEMMA, I WAS EXPECTING YOU BACK BY NOW – WAS MY BUDDHA BOWL NOT AS GOOD AS IT LOOKED? NICHOLAS x

Oh my gosh, it was him. My heart jumped a little, and suddenly I felt an urgent need to see him. I didn't want to look too keen, but I wasn't sure I could wait to reply – my fingers were already hovering over the keypad.

'Be cool Gemma!' I told myself, 'As cool as a Cucumber!'

Yet, even as I said the words, I knew how uncool I sounded.

'Be cool about what?' I jumped as Bronagh walked in.

She looked at the phone in my hands and grabbed it quick before I had even fully registered she was there.

'WHO is NICHOLAS?' She bellowed, eyebrows raised and huge smirk across her face.

'He's no-one!' I insisted, grabbing my phone back.

I could feel my face flaming, and I knew she would be able to read that reaction like a book.

'Uh huh!' She smirked again, 'So why are you turning into a beetroot?' She laughed aloud.

'I'm not!' I insisted, 'He's no-one. I barely even know him!'

'But clearly, you've thought about him naked!' She queried, clearly loving watching me squirm.

'I have not!!' I lied, instantly thinking about him naked.

'The lady doth protest too much, methinks.' She recited, giggling once more.

'Oh whatever!' I smiled and turned away from her glare, 'He is rather cute though.'

'Ooh I knew it, you little minx! Where did you meet him?'

'Just at one of these street food markets, with Martha.' I lied.

I pang of guilt hit me again.

'Oh, you hadn't said you'd been out with Martha recently?' She eyed me suspiciously.

'It was last week, remember? When you were too hungover to do anything? I popped into Martha after shopping, and we both fancied a change, so we nipped across to the market. Not long, just a quick bite of food and back – you know, get her out of the house for some air.'

'Ah lovely, and that brief flash of air has led to a little romance!' She chuckled.

'Well, I wouldn't say that exactly! Anyway, if you'll excuse me…'

'Er, I don't think so. You're not texting him straight back, are you?!' Bronagh actually sounded a little horrified.

'Er, well, it's been a few minutes.'

Bronagh roared with laughter.

'A few minutes. Even you can't believe that's being cool like a cucumber?' She laughed again, hard, and I poked her playfully in the ribs.

'Oi, stop making fun of me.' I chuckled a little too.

'Come on, give me that phone. We're going for one drink, give it an hour and then you can text him. Ok?' She asked.

'Ok!' I gave in, I knew no amount of protesting would work.

I followed Bronagh to the Student Union and we enjoyed a couple of casual drinks. True to her word, exactly one hour later she gave me my phone back. I'd had a missed call from my Mammy so decided to call her straight back before texting Nicholas.

'Hi Gemma.' Mammy spoke softly.

'Hi Mam, you ok?' I enquired.

'Yes sweetheart, I just miss you so wanted to call and see how you were?'

'Ah I'm fine thanks Mam, just out with Bronagh at the moment.'

'Lovely, say Hi for me, won't you?'

'I will Mam. I was actually wanting to pop home and see you soon?'

'Yes, I guessed you might do.'

'You did?' I was a little puzzled but starting to realise that nothing should surprise me anymore.

'Yes, just a feeling I had.' She explained.

'Right, ok,' Suddenly I wanted to see her right then and tell her what I knew, but I didn't want to alarm her either, 'Would Saturday suit you for me to visit?'

'Yes, of course! We'd be delighted to have you home – would you stay for the night and we can go to the pub like old times?' Her voice had a ring of excitement in it and I couldn't refuse.

'Yes, sounds lovely!' I confirmed.

'Right then, I'll tell you Dad to be ready. See you Saturday love.'

'See you Saturday Mam.'

I stood and looked at my phone for a minute and grinned. This news could change Mammy's life so much now – she would finally be able to unburden her secret on to me and live a little more freely. My heart swelled with love for her, and for the first time since leaving I was genuinely excited to have a visit back at home.

After my conversation with Mammy I had completely forgotten to respond to Nicholas, and I awoke the next morning with a start. It was immediately at the front of my mind, and I knew it was my magic setting me a reminder of what I needed to do first.

HI NICHOLAS, IT WAS THE BEST BUDDHA BOWL I'VE EVER HAD – I WILL DEFINITELY BE BACK FOR THAT, OR SOMETHING ELSE, SOON! GEMMA x

I pressed send before I could change my mind. I'd never been so cheeky in my life, and for the first time I understood what people meant when they said they felt like a naughty schoolgirl. Almost straight away a text message pinged back.

WOULD THAT SOMETHING ELSE BE FOOD RELATED? I'M NOT SURE I COULD KNOCK UP

ANYTHING AS GOOD AS THE BUDDHA BOWL. N x

I smiled, and longed to see both him and the Other World.

WELL I SUPPOSE THAT DEPENDS ON WHAT EXACTLY IS EDIBLE ON YOUR STAND?! G x

I cringed instantly at my cheesiness, but I was also enjoying being a bit naughty.

IT WILL BE INTERESTING WHEN YOU COME BACK AND TRY TO FIND OUT THEN! MAYBE SOME OF THE TASTE TESTING SHOULD TAKE PLACE AWAY FROM THE STAND? A PICNIC IN THE PARK MAYBE? N x

Was he asking me on a date? Eek, it seemed so!

THAT SOUNDS GREAT! WHEN? G x

I KNOW IT'S LATE NOTICE BUT HOW ABOUT THIS AFTERNOON? AROUND 3PM? N x

PERFECT, WHERE SHALL I MEET YOU? REMEMBER I'M NEW SO DON'T KNOW MANY PLACES. G x

I'LL MEET YOU AT THE ENTRANCE YOU ARRIVED IN THE OTHER NIGHT. SEE YOU AT 3! N x

Excitement filled me, I was going to see the Other World and Nicholas again! What would I wear? What would I say? I'd never been so excited about a date before, and I didn't want to appear an inexperienced fool. I need to remain calm, I thought, but even so I would check with Bronagh on the clothes.

A couple of hours later I was walking towards where I was meeting Nicholas, albeit a little earlier than I should have been. I knew I couldn't walk past Martha's house without saying Hello, so I tentatively gave her door a little knock.

'Hello Gemma!' She proclaimed as she opened the door, 'To what do I owe this visit?'

'I was just passing.' I explained, as we headed into her lounge.

'It's lovely out, shall we sit in the garden?' Martha enquired.

'Ooh that would be lovely. I do miss having a garden at Uni.' I sighed.

'How is University going? I keep meaning to ask, but with one thing and another we've been a bit distracted.'

'It's going good. Obviously, I got a little side-tracked recently, but after the other night I worked really hard to catch back up and with a little help I think I'm back on track.'

'That's great to hear my dear. You know, it's easy to get caught up in the madness, and forget that we are living actual real lives, so I'm pleased to hear that you haven't been distracted too far from your studies. They are very important.' Martha started to look around, 'I didn't get us a drink, did I?'

'It's no problem...' I started, but she wouldn't let me finish.

'Not at all, I will not have my guests going without some refreshments! That wouldn't be very hospitable of me!' She announced as she rose from her chair.

A couple of minutes later Martha was back with a large jug of yellow liquid, jingling about with plenty of ice.

'Freshly made lemonade, dear.' She told me, again like she'd read my mind.

'So, where exactly did you say you were off to?' Martha queried.

'Erm, actually I'm going back to the Other world.' I stuttered.

'For any reason in particular?' Martha had a glint in her eye that told me she knew exactly why.

'Er, well, yes…'

'Nicholas?' She enquired innocently, a slight grin on her face.

I nodded, and blushed. I really needed to learn to control that bodily function!

'He's a nice boy Gemma, make sure to relax and enjoy.'

I frowned.

'Is something wrong?' Martha knew me so well.

'I just can't help wondering, you know being magic… could he have, I don't know…'

'Put a spell on you?' Martha laughed.

'Well yes, not necessarily a spell, but you know, manipulated me somehow?' I felt slightly silly now I'd said it aloud.

'Well let me ask you this Gemma; When you first saw him, in those first few minutes, did you find him attractive?'

'I suppose I did, yes.'

'Well then, there's your answer.'

'Hmmm, I guess so.'

'Plus, one of the things magic has no power over is emotions. So, to answer your question, no – he couldn't have manipulated this in any way. Everything you are feeling is good, old fashioned lust. Now go, relax, and have fun!' Martha ordered.

And with that I stood and almost ran to the Other World.

17 DAY DATE

Nicholas was already waiting for me as I rounded the corner into The Other World. He didn't notice me at first, he was too busy fiddling with a button on his shirt. Gosh, he's even better than I remembered, I thought to myself as I took in his broad, strong shoulders and thick muscly legs. I paused and admired him for a few minutes and smiled to myself at how well I had done in getting this far with him. Before I came to London I had only been on one and a half dates – I'm not sure you can really count the second one as date, as his mom called halfway through to tell him his cat had died and I never saw him again, but I figured we had one drink together and so it must count as half a date? He must have took losing his cat really hard though, as he'd never responded to me after that. But other than that, I hadn't had much luck on the romantic front, I was just really awkward when it came to boys, and I had no confidence talking to them at all if I had even the slightest inclination of attraction to them. I would clam up and feel my face get warm and sticky, while I struggled to find words that didn't make me sound like a complete dork. I was absolutely fine with them if I had no romantic interest in them, I could talk all day about anything, but throw a bit of attraction into the mix and I was a bumbling fool. Things had gotten a little easier since coming to London, my confidence had inanely grown, and I felt a lot more self-assured these days when talking to anybody, not just hot men. I had met such an array of people since moving to the city that my conversation skills had grown immensely too. Actually, so had my listening skills which definitely helped. The more you listen to a person, and learn about them, the easier it is to feign interest and gain their friendship. Bronagh had taught me that, she'd taught me a lot of things. And with the new relaxed approach I had to making conversation, and a bit of courage usually in the shape of booze, I had started to feel more at ease talking to hot guys. I think that's how I'd lucked out on Nicholas, as he was THE hottest guy that had ever looked my way, and I knew that if I'd met him several months before there's no way I would have stayed cool enough to flirt with him, let alone come and meet him. I just prayed that I wouldn't lose it halfway through the date and start acting all weird, asking him about what his favourite boyband was, and the like.

Right in the middle of my pep talk to myself Nicholas caught sight of me and quickly forgot all about his half-closed button and grinned a huge genuine smile, with his perfect white teeth. I smiled right back and strolled over, breathing deeply to stay calm, and proceeded to unravel his button from some rogue cotton and slot it perfectly through his buttonhole for him. He blushed slightly, and for once I felt like I might be the more intrepid one of us.

'Hey.' I started.

'Hi! Er thanks for that.' He replied.

'No problem. How are you?' I asked.

'I'm good thank you, and you?' He responded.

'Yes, good thanks!'

I felt calm and ready for this date, I realised.

'Great – so listen, I was thinking… if it's ok with you, are you ok if we get out of here a little? I mean, not too far, I don't want to worry you, but I'd love to take you to this great park I know?'

He was clearly nervous, and now I was starting to feel it too.

'Er, sure. But isn't there a great park just down there?' I pointed towards the wannabe Central Park.

'Ah yeah, but that's so commercialised these days, I know somewhere much more beautiful if I may?'

I nodded, 'Sure!'

'Cool, it will only take us a few minutes to get to in the station and through the gateway if there are no queues, which there shouldn't be at this time!'

'Great, so where is it exactly we're going?'

'It's Other Giethoorn Village, it's in the Other Netherlands!' Nicholas smiled broadly at me.

'Huh?! The Netherlands?!' I was momentarily taken aback.

'Yes, the Other Netherlands…Is that too much for a first date?'

'I'm not sure… but anyway, how will we even get there? Do we need to fly? Can I leave the country with a man I've just met?' My mind raced away from my mouth.

'Gemma, you are in the Other world now remember…' Nicholas spoke softly, 'We don't need to fly. For travel here we have another kind of system. We just head to a station, similar to your airports, and queue for the destination you want. Once you've shown your ID and told them which part of the country you're heading to, then you merely need to walk through a door and a strange time travel thing happens so that you are instantly in the place you want to be.'

'Seriously?! Are you joking?'

'No, I'm not. This is real. But look, if you don't feel comfortable that's fine too… let's go to the park down the street…' He trailed off.

'No way! I need to see this time travel! And, I've always wanted to go to the Netherlands. I might just text Martha and let her know where I'm going, in case I get lost or stuck there or something, but yes – let's go!' I insisted.

We walked down the street for a mile or two and came to a fairly standard looking station.

'Is this it?' I questioned Nicholas.

'Yes, we're here.' He gazed at me, trying hard not to laugh.

'What?' I asked him.

'Nothing! It's just a long time since I've met someone with this level of wonder and amazement…it's endearing!' He beamed.

The station was nothing like what I was expecting. Despite Nicholas explaining that it was just like an Airport in the Real World, I had still fully expected it to be even a little bit special. In my head I had imagined a fairly normal looking station, but with all kinds of wizardy type walking through the walls. But I was sadly disappointed. There was nothing that looked even the slightest bit out of the ordinary. There were many screens displayed that detailed what platform was for what destination, however the platforms were more like departure gates at airports with people stood at desks in front of the doors, presumably checking ID and taking your exact destination, before the double doors swung open to let the next passengers through and then closing abruptly behind them. I was in awe as I saw all of the destinations on the board. I noticed that many of them were serviced by the same platform number and so I asked Nicholas about that. It's just so they don't need to have lots of platforms open when it's not busy, he explained, nothing more magical than that. We headed over to our platform and joined a short queue.

'So, this place we're going to...' I began.

'Mmmm?' He eyed me with amusement.

'What is it called again?'

'Other Giethoorn Village.'

'Great – and what's so special about it?'

'You'll see!' He winked and stepped forward to greet the lady at the checkout desk.

After a brief exchange she gestured us through. I was a little disappointed to find that, when I walked through the double doors and they closed behind me, another set opened in front and we walked straight through into the destination we'd chosen. There were no bright lights or vortex type experiences, which is what I'd anticipated. It all seemed very normal. It was painless though, I had to admit. I'd not travelled much, but from what I had experienced there was nothing worse than long queues for bag drop and check-in, followed by long queues at security, then long queues at the gate, all topped off with a long flight somewhere. Plus, the pain didn't end there. Once you'd got to your destination you then had to join a long queue for passport control, and then wait for what usually felt like a lifetime for the baggage carousel to start and once that was all done you had to find your way from the airport, which was usually in the middle of nowhere useful, to your actual destination. I've heard people talking about popping over to Ireland as it's only an hour on the plane, but in actual fact if you totalled up all of the travel to the airport, waiting around, queueing, flying and travelling to your landing-place you're probably talking closer to 5 hours. This, on the other hand, took us less than 5 minutes.

As we stepped outside the exit doors I was taken aback by the beauty of our surroundings. I'd never quite seen anything like it. The houses were stunning, large but with an old-fashioned feel, steepled in thatched roofs – quite similar to the houses in my Village back home, only much bigger and prettier. There were footpaths and bridges all around, but what was most peculiar was the water where the roads should be. There was literally no type of street for motorised vehicles. The only transport I could see were pushbikes and small boats. It was like a breath of fresh air, and it certainly made for a picture-perfect view.

'I tend to walk along the footpaths here, but if you'd prefer, we could get a boat bus?' Nicholas broke through my thoughts.

'A walk would be lovely.' I confirmed.

Nicholas gently took my hand and a ting of electricity ran up my arm. I'd never had someone hold my hand in this way before. Of course I'd held hands with my Mom and Dad when I was younger, and my friends on the playground – heck, I'd sometimes still hold hands with my friends on nights out these days, but that was usually more for support to stay upright. But this was the first time someone had ever held my hand in a romantic way, and it felt really nice. We strolled along in silence for a little while as I took in the view. This place was unbelievably beautiful, and it wasn't at all touristy. A real hidden gem. I'd need to tell Mammy about this place. She'd love it, I thought. The sun sat gently on my shoulders, filling me with warmth, and a slight breeze drifted past to create the perfect climate. I took some time to listen to the birds chirping smoothly from the trees and take a good look around at the surroundings. There were small boats drifting by frequently, filled with relaxed chatter, and people strolling by – just as slow and casual as we were. Nobody seemed to be in a particular hurry, and everyone seemed happy. It was a stark contrast to London, and just the respite I needed.

'The park is just over this way Gemma.' Nicholas guided me across a small bridge and into a small opening.

'Wow!' I gazed admiringly at the sight before us.

We entered what looked like a poppy field, that had small paths winding through and the occasional picnic table or blanket dotted about. The red colour of the poppy was vibrant against the green grass of the field, and it was an extraordinary thing to see in the flesh. Nicholas continued to lead me, and we found a small, clear patch on the ground in a quiet corner where he proceeded to open out his picnic blanket and lay it down. He gestured for me to sit as he sat down his basket and opened it up to reveal an array of delights.

'I wasn't sure what you liked, other than Buddha bowls, so I brought a selection.' He nervously explained.

'I'm sure it's great!' I replied encouragingly.

'It's quite basic.' He blushed.

'I love basic.' I smiled at him.

Nicholas proceeded to empty out the contents of his basket, and I saw that he'd packed fresh breads, cheeses, meats, chutney's and olives, along with a sweet selection of pastries, fruits and to finish it all off a box of chocolates.

'I couldn't think of anything else I would have chosen.' I told him encouragingly, and he beamed with a small glow radiating from his face.

'I also have this!' And he pulled a crisp cold bottle of Champagne from his bag, with some flute glasses along with some chopped Strawberries to go inside.

'Ooh, good thinking!' I told him, and I truly meant it.

In that moment, I had never felt more special to another person.

'Please tuck in.' Nicholas instructed, and I proceeded to help myself to the warm bread and cold meats.

'So, tell me a bit about yourself, Nicholas?' I enquired.

'Ha, straight to the point! What do you want to know?' He asked, chuckling to himself.

'I don't know, anything! Everything!' I laughed.

'Well, there's nothing very exciting to know. I grew up in Surrey with my parents and my sister. I'm studying at the moment to be a Vet, so I work part time for the Vendor where you met me, just a couple of evenings and weekends, and I love animals – especially Mice!'

'Mice?!'

'Yes – I love them. I can't wait until I finish my course and get a place with a garden so I can get a whole field of Mice!' He chuckled.

'Life goals right there!' I giggled.

'What about you?' Nicholas questioned back.

'Well, I am an only child. I grew up with both of my parents, and my Granny was not too far away – she's passed now though…' Nicholas gently touched my arm in sympathy, 'I live in the countryside but I moved to London to study and I love it.'

'So how did you come to find the Other World?' Nicholas pressed.

'Well I've always had a bit of a strange reaction to some things – I'd know when something bad was going to happen, or I'd get excited days before something good happened, that kind of thing. As I got older it did wear away a bit, but it never went away completely. I'd never taken much notice of it, but one day I got on the wrong tube, and I got off in a terrifying place. I was so scared of what I'd experienced, as it was nothing like I'd ever seen in the Real World before, but I started to wonder if I was going a little mad and it was all in my head. So, I went to speak with Martha, as she is my closest confidante in London and I knew she wouldn't judge me, and she advised me to look for a certain book. I suppose I relied on my instinct, or what I now know as my magic, to find this needle in a haystack book – and it led me, eventually, to the Visitor Centre.'

'When did all this happen?'

'Quite recently, within the last few weeks.'

'Oh wow, so you are a real newbie then!' He teased.

'Yes, I suppose I am,' I chuckled, 'How about you? How did you come to find it?'

'Well I've always known about it really. Although I grew up in the Real World, both my parents were raised in the Other World and so we visited frequently, and I live there now. All of my Grandparents still live in the Other World too. They don't see the point in living in the Real World, they tell me. Too much negativity apparently.'

'Well I can't say I disagree with them. But growing up weren't you confused? Didn't you ever want to bring your friends?'

'Yes, I did want to bring them. But my parents had instilled in me how I must never disclose it to anyone in the Real World, otherwise I could never get access to the Other World and visit my Grandparents again. And so, it became the norm for me. If we spent a weekend in the Other World, I would just tell my friends we'd been away for the weekend. My parents had invented a make-believe Caravan that they owned, and that's where we told anyone from the Real World where we'd been.'

'Gosh, that's amazing.' I told Nicholas.

'Hmmm, a little lonely at times though. I'm quite fortunate in that I have friends in both Worlds, but it can sometimes get a little tough managing between the two worlds. Everyone finds their way in the end though.'

'So how come you choose to still spend time in the Real World, and not live in the Other World full time? From what I've seen it looks amazing!'

'It is, but I also love the Real World. I like the feeling of accomplishment I get when I've had to put effort into something, which is harder to come by in the Other World. Plus, I love the education there, that's where I go to University, as there is no cheating with magic. But maybe one day I'll stick to one world!'

Over the course of the afternoon I learned all about Nicholas, and his experiences growing up, and he learned all about me. We chatted like we were the best of friends, and the time flew by. I'd never felt so comfortable in anyone's company, other than Bronagh's, and I wanted the time to slow down so I could savour every moment with Nicholas. We laughed about his geekiness in flirting skills, and he teased me about my apparent brashness. I told him that I was actually usually really shy, and he confided that he too was quite a shy personality. We clicked in every which way, and I'd never felt more at ease opening up myself to someone so honestly. I could have spent many more hours on the date, but as the time passed, the sun started to set, and the sky started to dim.

'I suppose we better get going soon.' Nicholas instructed, but hesitated to move.

'I guess we should,' I agreed, but again made no effort to move, 'I've had a really great time Nicholas, thank you.'

'Me too.' he replied, and with that he leant in and kissed me very gently on the mouth.

I looked at him, slightly surprised by this gesture, but then took the moment to reciprocate and leant back into him and kissed him slightly harder, and for slightly longer. I longed for more, but I knew that we would be seeing each other again very soon, I could feel it. We stood together, packed all of our belongings away and took a slow stroll, hand in hand back to the station.

'Can I see you again?' Nicholas nervously asked, not meeting my gaze, as we stepped out back in Other London.

'I'd really like that.' I nodded.

And with that Nicholas walked me all the way back to my door in the Real World and gave me long kiss goodnight before departing.

18 REVEALING ALL

The couple of days after meeting up with Nicholas passed in a blissful blur. We texted each other almost constantly when we weren't in lectures or sleeping, and I was keen to see him soon, but I knew I needed to make Mammy my priority first. I had promised her I would visit, and I also desperately wanted to let her know she could talk to me, confide in me, that I knew all about the Other World. I decided to travel up to her on the Saturday morning, partly because I had an assignment I wanted to get finished on the Friday evening so I could really enjoy my weekend, but partly because I knew Daddy would be at work on the Saturday morning so I could have a good chance to talk to Mammy.

My plan worked, when I arrived at home mid-morning on the Saturday Daddy was out at work and Mammy was in the middle of following a recipe along with a cooking show.

'Gemma, oh my sweet girl, come in – I've missed you!' Mammy showered me in kisses.

'I've missed you too Mam.' I hugged her warmly.

'Listen, let me just finish this recipe…' she told me, 'and I'll be with you'.

Mammy was a bit behind with the times and still had an old Terrestrial TV that couldn't pause or record, or access catch up. I had previously tried to talk her in to getting a digital box loads of times, but she wouldn't have it. She didn't need it, she told me. She either watched her programme or she didn't, there was nothing important enough that she needed to pause or record – she wouldn't be a slave to the TV. That was fine, but it meant that if she didn't follow her programme right now, she wouldn't be able to finish her recipe and that could leave her in a bit of a funny frame of mind for the rest of the day. I left her to get finished and wondered upstairs to my room to drop my belongings and take a shower. I'd lived in this house my entire life, but somehow things seemed different to me now. Aside from the fact that the everyday familiarity was gone, I started to look at things with a different eye. To get from my bedroom to the bathroom, I had to pass Mammy and Daddy's bedroom which was in the middle. The door was slightly ajar, and I glanced in as I passed. I was struck by a dream catcher hanging over the head of the bed. The dream catcher had been there for as long as I remembered, but suddenly it seemed a little strange to me. Mostly because I'd noticed them quite a lot in the Other World. Was there something magic about the dream catcher? There must be, I conceded, but how had I not questioned it before, I wondered, it was certainly a strange thing for Mammy to buy and put up – not really keeping with her traditional personality and character. I shook my head in confusion but continued my pursuit of the bathroom. As I turned on the shower and undressed, I proceeded to put my towel in the airing cupboard out of habit, as we always did. Mammy insisted we pop our towels in there whilst we washed to warm them up for when we came out, yet as I opened the door, I noticed it wasn't particularly warm inside to heat the towels up. I'd never really noticed it before, I suppose because I'd had no need to query it, but I thought about it as I sudded myself up and washed myself down. No matter how hard I tried to get it out of my mind, it was really bugging me, so I jumped out of the shower a little bit sooner than I'd intended and opened the airing cupboard back up. It still wasn't warm inside, yet my towel was heated to a perfect temperature to suit the slightly breezy morning. Now I thought about it the towels always came out at the perfect temperature to suit the weather. They always felt quite cool in the summer but lovely and hot in the winter. Was this Mammy's magic, I wondered? How had I never thought this unusual before?

After I had dried myself down, I opened my wardrobe for something to wear and noticed that all of my clothes hanging inside were perfectly ironed. Again, this wouldn't have surprised me ordinarily, Mammy was adamant that we were well turned out and wore clean, smart clothes at all times, which inevitably led to all of our clothes being ironed to precision by Mammy before being put away, but I noticed that even the clothes that I'd just pulled out of my bag all crumpled now looked exceptionally wrinkle free. Has Mammy been filling this house with magic the whole time and Daddy and I have never noticed? She must have been. Come to think about it, I've never actually seen her doing any ironing – I'd always just assumed she'd done it whilst we were out in the day. Surely, I couldn't have spent all of those years here, amongst magic, and not taken any notice of any of it?!

I wondered downstairs to ask Mammy. As I entered the kitchen, she was just putting her pie in to the Oven.

'Just in time Gemma, I'm all finished for an hour!' Mammy beamed.

I felt a little bit indignity that Mammy had been using magic right under my nose and expecting me not to notice. I was a little bit offended and felt myself stepping back in to one of my teenage tantrums.

'Have you even turned the oven on?!' I stropped sarcastically, but Mammy didn't notice my accusatory tone.

'Of course, I have dear, how do you think I'd cook the dinner?' She asked innocently.

'Probably the same way you warm our towels or iron our clothes…' I declared, 'Who knows what else you've been doing?'

Mammy roared with laughter, not exactly the kind of response I was expecting, and I raised my eyebrows in bewilderment.

'Oh Gemma, Martha told me that you know. I've heard all about how you found out and spoke with Malachy and had a little night out with Martha to her and Granny's hotspot.'

'You know?!'

'Of course, I do! Did you think Martha wouldn't tell me?'

'Well, I suppose I didn't think about it. I thought we couldn't tell people?'

'We can't tell people that don't know Gemma, that's why I've never been able to tell you. Plus, I wasn't sure if you were meant for it. Obviously, I'm absolutely delighted that you know now, but you can't be cross with me for not talking to you about it – I couldn't!'

I felt myself softening a little to Mammy. I did understand that she couldn't have told me, although I still felt a bit embarrassed that it had been right under my nose without me knowing anything out of the ordinary was going on. But I knew she was just making life a little easier for her, and not trying to make fools of Daddy or me.

'No, I get it Mam. I'm sorry!' I gave her a big hug.

'I'm sorry too – you know if I could have told you I would have!' She declared.

'I know, I know. Ignore me!'

'So, tell me all about how you've been finding it!' Mammy insisted.

Mammy and I spent the afternoon talking about all things magic and Other world. I was amazed by some of her stories and it made me see a whole new side to her. She lit up when she talked about her experiences, and abilities and I felt a pang of sympathy for her that she's had to live with it hidden for so long. However, when we talked about it she wasn't sad, she explained her love for Daddy, and then myself, was so much stronger than anything she felt for magic and she has never once regretted her decision to live solely in the Real World in order to live a life with us. She also told me how she could still freely visit the Other world if she wanted to, but she didn't want to live any of her life without being able to talk freely to Daddy about it, she would feel deceptive to him, and so it has been totally her decision to not go to the Other world any longer. I was right in my uncovering of the bits of magic she still uses around the house, turns out she was quite gifted magically, and she still uses it a little to make her life easier – but never enough to provoke any suspicion and she is happy with that. Mammy also told me that she had thought about telling Daddy a number of times, but she wasn't sure he'd understand or even fully believe her, and she didn't want to risk being blocked from magic in case it ever impacted on me finding out, should I be destined for it. So, much to Granny's disappointment, Mammy decided to live a 'normal' life in the Real world. And she loved her life, she told me, and wouldn't change a thing. My heart swelled with pride and love for the woman I could now see clearly before me, and I suddenly had a true appreciation for what a remarkable woman she was. I also felt like I'd met a whole new persona to Mammy, and I had the most amazing afternoon getting to know her all over again. By the time Daddy got home we were curled up on the loungers in the back garden, drinking crisp white wine and laughing about long forgotten tales of Mammy's younger years.

'Well Hello you two!' Daddy beamed at us, 'You certainly look like you're having fun!'

'Yes, I suppose we are.' Mammy grinned a huge smile.

It had been a long time since I'd seen her so animated.

'You'll have to come home more often Gemma; it seems to be having a great effect on your Mother!'

'Er, what about you? Aren't you pleased to see me?' I teased.

'Oh er, of course!' Daddy flustered.

'I'm joking Dad, come here and give me a hug!'

I felt more at ease with Mammy and Daddy and my home than I ever had done. I realised that I'd always had a slight unfamiliarity with my surroundings there, that I'd never quite noticed before, and now it was like I had fully opened my eyes and recognised everything. I felt more relaxed in this world, now I understood myself, and I had gained a fresh assurance from it. Daddy sat down and joined us for a drink, something he very rarely did at home, and he too seemed comfortable and confident. He was full of the joys and spent time filling us in on all of the Village gossip and happenings. Mammy and I were having a wonderful time listening to Daddy regaling his tales, and this made him more content with talking to us. I don't think there had ever been a time that we'd all been so at ease, and taken so much enjoyment, from each other's company.

We spent Saturday evening in the pub, as usual, and I enjoyed seeing all of my old friends and acquaintances and enjoyed the ease and familiarity of being home. I went to bed happy and carefree, and smiled as I thought to myself that I'd never been this content in life before.

I woke up on Sunday to the wonderful smell of food frying, the smell wafted through the house and up to my bedroom. Mmmm, I stretched out and wished I could stay longer. I never thought that would be something I'd ever wish for, but with my knew found knowledge of Mammy suddenly the home seemed different, in a good way, and I was truly enjoying my time here. I headed downstairs to the sound of Daddy humming along to the radio, and watched as he busied himself in the kitchen, cooking the breakfast, as Mammy bustled around setting up the outside table for us to eat at. I stood still momentarily, to study them while they were unaware they were being watched so were acting all natural, and I saw how truly happy they were. Not that I'd ever thought they were unhappy, but watching them liaise with each other, after 25 years of marriage and still so in love I realised I genuinely understood Mammy's decision to give up magic for love. They say true love is a once in a lifetime thing, and I couldn't imagine that Mammy would have found anyone else whom she loved so greatly, who adored her in return.

'Ah Gemma, just in time.' Daddy called as he caught sight of me.

'Come on dear, come and sit with your old Mam outside.'

I headed out and took a seat with Mammy.

'I've got all your favourites love.' Daddy shouted.

'Thank you!' both Mammy and I replied in unison, then turned to one another and laughed.

'I've got all of both your favourites, my wonderful girls.' Daddy told us placing down our breakfasts.

'Oh Dad, you even sprung for the good sausages!' I exclaimed excitedly.

They were my favourites and I was delighted he'd made a special effort to get them in for me.

'I did indeed. I need something to keep enticing you back, so you don't completely forget us in the big city!'

'Ah would I ever?!' I grinned and tucked into my huge breakfast.

I decided to head back to London shortly after my breakfast, to make sure I was back in plenty of time to get all my notes and assignments sorted for the week ahead. I had some exams coming up and I couldn't afford to fall behind again, especially if I wanted to see Nicholas anytime soon. Which I did. Daddy tried to insist on driving me back to London, but I convinced him that I wanted to get the train so I could do some work.

Truth was I wanted to catch up on texting Nicholas. Luckily Daddy didn't question my reasonings and agreed to drop me to the station. The journey back was uneventful, and I reflected on the wonderful week I'd had. Before I came to London, I could never have imagined my life would ever be this amazing, or that I would ever feel this fulfilled. But finally, I was starting to feel genuinely excited for my future, and everything that lay ahead for me.

19 DISCOVERING

I arranged to meet Nicholas again the next weekend. I wanted it to be sooner, but I couldn't miss any more of my lectures plus I didn't want to make Bronagh any more suspicious than she already was, so I spent a quiet week going to lectures and getting my coursework up to date and to a good standard. Come Saturday morning I was filled with a restless energy. I woke up quite early, which was obviously a sign of having a quiet week with very little alcohol, and wondered what I could do with myself for the few hours before I went to the Other World. I wasn't meeting Nicholas until mid-afternoon and I wasn't sure if I could keep myself occupied for long enough to not drive myself completely insane with agitation. I pulled out my phone and started to flick through various contacts. It wasn't very often that one of my usual friends wasn't around, also looking for something to do, but a group of them had decided to do a day trip out to one of the nearby National Trust places. It was only me and Susie who made our excuses, as I was meeting Nicholas and Susie was heading home for the weekend. Our whole dorm was pretty much empty, with everyone enjoying a sun filled Saturday outside. As a distraction I started skimming over all of the photos on my phone, smiling at the various memories, before I came across the images I had taken from the book in the library. It felt like a lifetime ago since I'd found it, and discovered the other world, but in reality, it was only a few weeks ago. I hadn't even thought about the other entrances much, instead I'd stuck to the one on Martha's street as it was the easiest. I glanced through the images and wondered where the other entrances would take me. There were plenty in London, especially through the disused tube stations. I was weary of these ones after the terrifying experience that I'd had the first time, however Nicholas had explained to me that these kind of protectors were merely put up to guard the Other World against unwanted visitors, and they only disappear when people have an idea about why they are there and stop demonstrating fear. This made sense alongside what Martha had told me initially about not being afraid, but I was still hesitant. However, the more I looked over the various entrances, the more I realised that the tube stations were by far the easiest and most convenient way to get across. It seemed that the London Underground had a whole host of Ghost Stations, and most of these now acted as a gateway to the Other World. What if I went there now, and wondered around by myself for a while, I thought? I could spend some time exploring before I met Nicholas. I'd only ever been to the Other World with people, since I'd first been to the Visitor Centre, and I longed to see more. I checked my watch and I had a fair few hours before I was due to meet Nicholas, and one of the abandoned tube stations was just around the corner from my dormitory, so I decided to go for it – go and explore a little on my own.

I approached the tube station slowly, as I wasn't sure where exactly the entrance was. This tube station wasn't in use at all anymore, like the last one had been, it had been completely shut many years previous and instead another tube station had opened just next door. There was a bar situated on the other side of the entrance, but as it was early the only people inside were the staff who were setting up ready for the mid-morning brunch crew. I hovered outside the old entrance, and pretended I was looking at a map on my phone and looking around confused like I wasn't sure where I was going and was just trying to find my bearings. Ordinarily this may have attracted unwanted attention from helpful passers-by offering directions, but I knew I would be safe to avoid this kind of attention in London. Nobody wants to help here, they're all too busy being important and fabulous of course. As I leaned against the side of the entrance, I could see that some of it had been boarded up, but an iron shutter was also pulled across, which was obviously how they had used to shut the station up previously. I gave a slight pull on the shutter, but it didn't budge. I didn't want to attract too much attention so I walked to the other side of the entrance, pretending I was trying to read a street sign, so that I could look at it from another angle. Bingo, I thought as I saw it. I small wedge in the side of the wood showed that it wasn't quite closed properly, and I would be able to get through. I waited until the street was relatively empty and slipped inside. I rushed out of sight and when I was sure no-one could see me, I stopped to look around. It reminded me very much of the platform at Charing Cross, which had taken me to the Other World. The initial entrance was typical of the underground, very dark and quite dirty, but once you'd passed out of sight from the Real World the station became lovely, bright and inviting. Must be the magic, I thought. I headed down the only corridor and through a small doorway on to a platform. There was an older man stood there who looked rather surprised to see me.

'Ah, Hi!' He said, slightly bewildered, 'Er, did you follow me down here?' He shifted uncomfortably.

'Oh no!' I insisted, 'I know where I'm going!'

'Right, ok, good! Well then I hope you have a lovely day.' He spoke, still a little uncertain.

'You too!' I smiled broadly.

Just then the tube pulled into the station and we got on different carriages to ensure the awkwardness ended as abruptly as it had started. I sat down and watched out of the window, curious to see if the passages looked the same as they did on the normal underground. I was slightly disappointed to see that they did, but the tube did seem to be moving at a much faster past. We were almost flying through the tunnels, but as I started to feel a bit of alarm rising inside me, the tube slowed again and ground to a halt. The familiar announcement called out that the train was now terminating, and all passengers were to change here, and I noticed quite a few people were now departing. I was a little surprised by the amount of people who had made the journey, alongside me, from the Real World to the Other World. Although I had seen many people whilst I had been in the Other World, and I now understood that it is more common knowledge than I initially thought, I still hadn't been expecting quite so many people to be making the same journey as me, especially not at the same time. I had assumed that it was all very secretive, very cloak and dagger, and that people tried to hide their passing, but it seemed to not be the case on this busy Saturday morning.

I exited the station and was pleased that this time there was no darkness, no scary sounds and nothing at all out of the ordinary. I looked around and decided to just have a stroll and see where I ended up. The station had brought me out on to a bustling main street, that was filled with shops and cafes, and I walked along delighted to feel that I felt familiar here now. The shops were lovely and reminded me of the kind of high streets you would find in years gone by. There wasn't a chain or department store in site, instead quaint boutiques lined the streets each with beautiful window baskets to decorate the area. The buildings were old, but extremely well cared for, and I guessed that I was in one of the older parts of the Other World. As I walked along, I spotted an old book store across the road and wondered over to take a look. Inside was a breath-taking sight, with the walls literally lined from floor to ceiling with bookcases and a huge spiral wooden staircase that was intricately carved dominating the corner of the room. The staircase, I noted, took you to different walkways across the bookcases, making accessibility easy, and the whole of the ground floor was filled with nooks and crannies, decorated with comfy cushions to sit and read on. I stood in awe for a while and didn't even notice a petite old lady make her way over to me.

'Can I help you my dear?' The old lady croaked.

'Yes, I wonder if you can…' I looked down at her, 'I'm quite new here, and I was wondering if you had any books that might help me learn more?'

The old lady chuckled.

'Of course I do! Now let me see. Hmm, I think the books about the feeling sense are up on the top shelves. Are you ok to go up there by yourself?'

'Yes, that's fine. But can I ask, what do you mean by the books about the feeling sense?'

'All of our books are about the different magic we possess. Yours is the feeling sense, so I assumed you'd want to read up on that?' She looked at me a little puzzled.

'The feeling sense, right. But, why do you assume that's my ability? It's just, I'm not sure yet…'

'Ah my dear,' She chuckled again, 'That's my job!'

'Right, ok. Well, thank you!' I started to head off.

'And…' She called after me 'There are a few books up there that will give you a basic history too, if you wanted them.'

'Yes, I do! Thank you so much.' And I carried on up.

There were thousands of books about the feeling sense up on the shelves, and I had no idea which one to choose. I scoured the shelves waiting for something to jump out at me, and it did, literally. Just as I was shuffling along a book wiggled out from the others and right into my hands. I looked at it and instantly recognised why it was for me.

THE FEELING SENSE – HOW TO USE IT AND CONTROL IT by ELSIE JONES

I decided to take the book with me and read it somewhere outside, as it was such a beautiful day, and I paid for it along with another book I'd found about the 'Becoming of the Other World' and thanked the old lady for all of her help before stepping back on to the street. The High Street was small, and I figured I could walk either way and be off it quickly, so I turned and walked the way I had been going, before I ended up in the bookstore. It didn't take me long to get to a small side street with a sign for The Visitor Centre. I wonder if it's moved for me, I thought, so I headed down in the direction the sign pointed to and sure enough came across the Visitor Centre. I walked back towards the stunning entrance and noticed a huge antique clockface on the front of the building that I didn't remember noticing last time. It told me that a couple of hours had passed since I'd left home, but I'd still got time before I met Nicholas, so I carried on inside the entrance. The hallway was different this time. There was no visitor book, or chair beside it, instead stood a huge grand entrance, with sweeping stairs to both sides and a beautiful chandelier hanging from the double levelled ceiling nearly all the way down to my height. The chandelier started at the ceiling with a thick base and spiralled down, getting narrower and narrower until it became a point. It was covered in an array of perfect, fluffy feathers and overshadowed everything else about the entrance hall.

'Gemma, I thought I might see you today!'

I turned and saw Malachy walking through the door I had just entered through. I realised I was really pleased to see him again.

'Malachy, this entrance hall is magnificent!' I declared.

'Yes, well I am rather pleased with it.' He smiled.

'It is definitely fit for a first timer now!'

'Oh no, Gemma, this isn't for the first timers. No, the old entrance hall is still for them, well with a little tweak of colour here and there. We can't have them feeling too intimidated when they first come here! Also, we need them to sign in and the visitor book just wouldn't fit with this decorum.' He explained.

'So, the first timers see a different entrance hall to everyone else?' I wasn't sure I'd understood.

'Exactly right – I always knew you'd be a fast learner.' He winked and walked off down the hallway.

I quickly followed behind and through another set of double doors that took us out on to the patio we'd sat at last time. We sat in the same huge cushioned seats and I noticed an iced tea appear in front of me today. I hadn't thought of asking for one, but now that I had it, I realised how much I wanted one. It was cold and slid down my throat with ease. I eyed Malachy as he also downed a glass of something cold, but his was a darker colour than mine and I wasn't sure exactly what it was.

'Well then Gemma, what can I do for you today?' Malachy asked.

'Nothing really, I don't suppose.' I looked at him and he laughed.

'Now there's an honesty you don't hear every day!'

I grinned at him and continued with my drink.

'I suppose I do have a few questions.' I told him.

'Please, go ahead…' He instructed me.

'I'm not sure if you know, but my Mammy has magic too.'

'Yes, I do know that.' He smiled.

'I noticed she uses magic in her house, but Daddy doesn't have magic – I guess, I didn't think this was allowed?'

'Why yes Gemma, you can use your magic in the Real World.

We advise it is limited, to avoid suspicion, and it may only be used for good, but otherwise yes - you can.'

'Right, I see. And the lady in the bookstore down the street told me that my magic is the sense of feeling, is that right?'

'Ha ha, you mean Mrs Birchall? Yes, she is correct. She is always correct – it is one of her senses, being able to pick up on other people's senses and abilities. She has a remarkable ability for it.'

'Oh perfect, I've got some books so I will read up on it. Would I have any other senses or abilities?'

'We're all made up of many truths, Gemma. Your feeling sense is your dominant one, however it is like any abilities you have in life, you can work on them if you put the effort in and choose to make them great.'

'Any of them I choose?'

'Yes. Think of school – you were very good at English, but not so good a Science correct?'

'Yes…' How did he know?!

'Well that is the same for everyone. Not necessarily in those subjects, but we all have things we are better at than others. However, if you'd had a real keen interest in Science and put a lot of study and effort into it, you almost certainly would have done better with it. Magic is the same. We all have areas where our natural ability lies, yet that doesn't always coincide with where our natural interest lies. It is certainly possible to work on other areas that you may be interested in, although I would advise you to focus on one area at a time and once that is mastered move on to the next.'

'I understand, thank you.'

'Anything else I can help you with?'

'There is one small thing actually. I just don't want to sound naïve or silly?'

'That is what I am here for. There's nothing I haven't heard before, over the years.'

'It's just that I saw a couple of wands for sale in the bookstore… I just assumed that wands were part of magic fiction?'

'Ah – they are, and they aren't. We are capable of magic without wands, it is controlled by our minds and senses. However, wands were invented to throw magic and keep its strength when doing so. We can send magic, but the wands accelerate the speed it gets there, and so it retains most of its strength. It isn't often we need to use them though Gemma, so I wouldn't be getting yourself one just yet.'

'Right, thank you! And what about spells and potions?'

'They exist. They aren't as necessary as the tales would have you believe, but they do have their uses.'

'I see, thank you Malachy – I really appreciate you taking the time to see me last minute!'

'Always a pleasure Gemma – and remember, use magic responsibly but don't forget to enjoy it!' And with that he was gone.

20 DISCOVERING MORE

I was waiting for Nicholas, book in hand, when he arrived. I'd headed straight for the closest café when I'd left the visitor centre, and text Nicholas to tell him to meet me there instead. I'd then settled myself down on a little bistro set outside on the terrace and quickly became engrossed in my book. I didn't even notice Nicholas when he arrived, I was so enthralled by everything I was learning.

'Hey.' He jolted me from my thoughts.

'Oh hey, sorry! I didn't even notice you arrive!' I apologised.

'That's ok – what are you reading?' He proceeded to look at the cover.

'It's a book, by my Granny! Turns out I have the same magic ability as her, but she was some amazing expert in it – the best in her field the book claims! So, I've been starting to learn all about my magic sense so that I can start to get to know it and use it more.'

'That's great Gemma, let me know if I can help at all.'

'I will do. What's your ability?' I queried, realising I actually had no idea.

'Ah, erm, I'm not sure you'd want to know.' Nicholas shifted uncomfortably, not meeting my gaze.

'Of course, I do, why would I possibly not want to know?' I was confused at his reaction.

'Look Gemma, just know that it is very tightly regulated, and can only be used for certain things…' He trailed off.

'Come on Nicholas, just tell me. You're making me nervous.'

'I have Mind ability. It means that I can read other people's minds, and I can put my thoughts in to their minds.'

'Wow.' I didn't know what else to say.

'I can't do it with everything, and you have to believe that I would never do it for any harm – or to encourage any romantic happenings, if you catch my drift.'

We both blushed slightly. I was keen to know more, but I didn't want to push Nicholas too hard at the moment. He clearly felt uncomfortable, and I trusted that he hadn't used his magic to influence me in any way, so I decided to drop the subject for now.

'Where are you taking me today?' I chirped.

'I'm actually not sure, in all honesty. I did think of a few places, but I wanted to ask if there's anywhere you really wanted to go first?'

My heart swelled slightly. Nicholas was so kind and thoughtful; he really was a good guy. I felt extremely fortunate to, not only have him as a date, but to also have him as a guide for this crazy new adventure I was on.

'Well I don't really know anywhere…' I paused momentarily, 'But I would love to go somewhere magic.'

'You are somewhere magic.' Nicholas explained slowly.

'No, I don't mean just magic as in here. I mean like a bit out there magic. Wacky magic. Not over the top insane, but just somewhere a bit special from magic, if there is such a place?'

'Of course, there is, there are places with every kind of magic touch from normal to insane…' He laughed, 'How about another park, but a lot less natural and a bit more magically made, where we can lie on the grass but also buy some beers?'

'Sounds perfect!' I smiled.

It didn't take us long to get there. It turns out that Other London is much like Real London in that it attracts people from all walks of like, all with different wants and expectations. This meant the city had been built on a foundation of multi-culturalism, and in the Other World this had resulted in some weird and wonderful places. The park Nicholas took me to was right in the middle of Other Notting Hill, so it was always going to be vibrant and colourful. It stood proudly in the middle of the area and you instantly knew you were walking into it by the bright yellow pathways and rose covered archway holding up a multicoloured sign that showed the entrance. Just inside the entrance was what appeared to be a lollipop patch, where people of all ages were helping themselves to an array of lollies. I was filled with excitement in the pit of my stomach as we walked in, this place could only be described as completely bonkers, but in a good way, and it was just what I wanted to see. Nicholas looked at me and smiled, and I grinned right back to let him know that this was a brilliant choice. We walked, hand in hand, along the yellow path until we reached a centre point, where the paths split off and became a mix of different colours, and the area in front of us was filled with loud and bright wooden huts that offered everything from food to drinks to ice creams and even blankets and parasols. There were tables and chairs for people to sit and eat but most of the visitors seemed to be dotted around the grass on various blankets. The paths, Nicholas explained to me, each went to a different area of the park and the colours were linked to a colour coding system which we found on a nearby sign. We walked the path to the river, and I was slightly dumbfounded. The trees glinted extremely brightly in the sun, and I stared at them intently for a while, trying to figure out what made them so vibrant.

'Is that… glitter?' I questioned Nicholas.

He laughed.

'Yes probably!' He followed my gaze and looked hard at the tree.

The trees seemed to have a sprinkling of glitter on the leaves and petals, which made them pop beautifully, and the trunks seemed to have patches of a kind of matted foil. It was very subtle, and merely enhanced the natural beauty of the trees.

'It's amazing.' I stared at it in wonder.

'If you think they're pretty take a look at the river.' Nicholas pointed ahead.

The river was a perfect shade of turquoise blue, like the kind of colour you see on pictures of the sea, in the most exotic of places. The kind of places I always longed to travel to but hadn't had the opportunity. The most calming shade of bluey green you could imagine and floating all across the top were bright pink buds that had fallen into the water.

'Oh goodness. I don't know what to say, it's stunning!' I was instantly in love with this park.

'It is very pretty.' Nicholas agreed.

'But where are the trees that the blossom has fallen from?' I looked around.

'I don't think there are any, I think they are just put there by magic because it's aesthetically pleasing.' Nicholas shrugged.

We found a patch of grass close by to the river's edge where we lay Nicholas' trusty picnic blanket down and sat watching the world go by for a while. People of all ages and interests filled the park. It also seemed that magic was more freely used here, as I saw people turning their lukewarm bottles of wine icy cold, beckoning the tree branches over so that they were more shaded and even sweeping their remnants away in to a bag, ready to be taken to a bin. I was mesmerised by the volume of people in this park alone that lived with magic. Could I live in the Other World I considered? As if by magic Nicholas broke through my thoughts.

'I'm not sure it would be that great living in this area full time.' He stated.

I looked at him, eyes narrowed in a questioning expression.

'What?' He questioned.

'Did you just read my mind?' I teased him.

'What?! No! Did I? I didn't mean to, honestly!' He fumbled for his words, and I laughed.

'It's fine!' I told him.

'No, but I really didn't mean to!' He explained.

'Maybe you didn't, maybe it was coincidence…' I reasoned.

'Maybe. Sometimes it happens to me unwittingly. Usually I have to concentrate on doing it, but it has been known to happen to me with people I have a connection to, and I don't realise it. I'm sorry Gemma!'

'It's fine honestly. I'm only teasing you anyway.'

'I promise it's never happened with anything serious. Like I wouldn't know if you were thinking you loved me or anything like that.'

We both blushed. I gently touched his arm.

'It's ok Nicholas. I trust you with my thoughts,' I laughed, 'Besides, if you ever did get access to something really personal, I'd be able to tell anyway.'

'How so?'

'Because you'd end up a right bumbling fool!' I roared with laughter.

'Oh, ha ha!' He joked, and gently nudged me in the ribs, 'So I'm a bit awkward when I'm uncomfortable, that can only be a good thing yeah?'

'It can only be.' I winked.

'Right, I'm going to get us some much-needed drinks to kill this conversation!' Nicholas declared, jumping to his feet.

'Right. In that case, I'll have something fruity please.'

'Something fruity alcoholic, or something fruity sensible?' He raised his eyebrows in question.

'Alcoholic please!' I smiled back.

'Great, I'll be back as quick as I can.' And with that he lent down and kissed my cheek before turning and walking away towards the huts.

I lay back and closed my eyes, enjoying the hum of a small duo practicing a chorus from a chart song not too far away from where we were sat. As Nicholas returned, I noticed he was clutching a huge sharing platter of nachos, as well as the drinks, and suddenly I wanted nothing more in the world than those cheese covered, sauce drenched nachos.

'Can you read minds even before they've thought things?!' I joked.

'Now that would be some skill! A good choice in the Nachos then?' He enquired.

'The best!' I told him, as I tucked in.

The afternoon passed by quickly, and easily, much like our first date had. We chatted like we'd known each other forever. I learned a bit more about Nicholas magic, and that of his Mom and Dad, and I told him a bit more about Mammy's magic. He was amazed by Mammy's dedication to Daddy, and we talked about the power of true love conquering all else. We discussed Granny and Martha, and we both spent some time talking about our studies and our hopes for the future. Mine were a little more lost now that I'd uncovered this new found world and ability, but I knew Nicholas was right when he told me to keep on as planned for now and I could always change my mind when I was sure of what path I wanted to take. Nicholas gave me some advice on practising my magic safely in the real world, and he also taught me a couple of tricks like how to give my skin a glow for those days, usually hungover ones, when I wasn't feeling most confident. I realised at the end of the date how much I did love spending time with Nicholas, and how attached I was starting to become to him. I wanted him to meet my friends and know a bit about my Real life, and I wanted to see more about his life, so I asked if he would consider a 'normal' date with me.

'What's a normal date?' He asked puzzled.

'Like in the Real World. Maybe you could come to my local pub with me one of the evenings with my friends?'

'I'd love that!' He beamed sincerely.

'Fab. We always go on a Wednesday, if you're free?'

'I'm supposed to be working but let me see if I can swap a shift.' He replied.

'I'll keep my fingers crossed.' And I hoped really hard that he could.

As we packed up and looked around to make sure we hadn't forgotten anything I noticed a girl watching us. She looked familiar and I realised that she was the girl I'd met in pretend Central Park that day, who had served me the sandwich.

'Hi!' I shouted over, startling her from her thoughts.

'Hi.' She mumbled, quickly busying herself with something else.

I saw Nicholas look up and his face flush with colour. As she turned to leave, she looked right at us and called over to us, 'Bye Nicholas, nice to see you.'

I turned to look at him, but he didn't meet me eye.

'Is she a friend?' I asked gently.

'Hmm, something like that.' He responded, and I could tell by his tone that he didn't wish to discuss it any further

'Let's go then.' He continued and briskly started to walk away.

I was confused, but quickly Nicholas was back to his chirpy, caring self and I forced myself to push all thoughts of the strange girl to the back of my mind, it wasn't the right time to push for answers. And it could have been nothing. Maybe she'd just been staring at me because she wasn't sure where she knew me from. I do that all the time, find myself watching people out of recognition but with uncertainty where I know them from. I've even had people ask me on a couple of occasions what I am looking at, so it must have been that. And then she realised she knew Nicholas so was being polite, I convinced myself. I soon forgot all about her and enjoyed the last bit of time I had with Nicholas today, turning my mind back to Wednesday and the quiet hope I was filled with that he could get out of work and come out with me to meet my friends.

21 HELLO THERE

To my utter delight Nicholas did actually make it to the pub with us on Wednesday, and the evening went better than I could have hoped for. All of my friends loved Nicholas and he in turn was charming and friendly and seemed to be having fun with them. Even Bronagh was on her best behaviour, which I hadn't been sure she would as she has a habit of giving guys a particularly hard time and watching them squirm. However, she seemed a bit softer towards Nicholas and I was glad, I didn't want her frightening him off. The evening was filled with plenty of drinks and laughter, but inevitably talk changed to our Summer plans after a few drinks. It was only a couple of weeks now until we broke for summer and there was a 7-week gap until we were due back to lectures.

'So…' Bronagh turned serious and dominated attention, 'What is everyone doing for the Summer?'

'I'm going home.' Susie piped up.

'Right, well that rules her out!' Bronagh smirked.

'Ruled me out for what?' Susie demanded.

'A couple of months of Summer city fun!' Bronagh teased, 'And also the chance to flat share with yours truly!'

'Have you got a flat sorted?' I asked quickly.

'Not yet, but I've booked in to view some later this week – you interested?'

'I am.' I nodded.

'I'm definitely in!' Joined Becks, 'My dorm mates are talking about us all sharing, but I can't deal with them for another month, let alone another year!'

'Ok but be warned my sister has decided to flat share with me too!' Bronagh informed us.

'Sister?' I queried, 'I didn't know she was moving to London.'

'Neither did I. But apparently, she is. Needs to be closer to job opportunities or something.' Bronagh rolled her eyes.

'Great – well I'm not sure what I'm doing through the Summer but I'm happy to pay for my room so I can keep it free and move in September.' I squirmed as I said it.

'WHAT?' Bronagh and Nicholas screeched at me together.

I frowned, not sure what to tell them.

'You're moving home for the Summer?' Nicholas asked more gently this time.

'Maybe – Daddy is expecting me back to work in the shop. It's tourist season, he needs the help.'

'I see.' Nicholas looked a little downcast.

'You can't!' Bronagh declared abruptly.

'Huh? Why?'

'You just can't. We need you here. Get a summer job here and stay. Your Dad will understand.'

'I'll see…' I cut her off, ready for a change in conversation.

'Why are you going home?' Becks asked Susie.

'Ah you know, my old Nan isn't well, and I just want to spend some time with her. Plus, my Dad gives me money for shopping if I'm there, whereas he seems to forget when I'm not!' Susie smiled coyly.

She was from a semi-wealthy family and being away from her family's home, complete with all the luxuries that came with it, was a bit hard on her. I wasn't at all surprised that she was heading back.

'What about you Nicholas?' Susie asked innocently.

'Me?' Nicholas looked surprised to be caught off guard.

'Yes, you!' Susie chuckled.

Everyone turned to look.

'Well, I'll be staying in the city. I already have work and a place to live.'

'Oh, where do you actually live?' Stacey joined in the inquisition.

'Erm, it's outside of the city, I'm not sure you would have heard of it…' He trailed off.

'Oh no, can you still get the tube where you are?' Bronagh enquired, 'Like, it's not so far that the tube doesn't even go there, and you need to get the over ground?' she feigned a horrified expression.

'Ha, no, it's not that far out. Just a little past Epping.'

'Oooh.' We all mouthed together.

'At least you can still get there easy enough.' Becks encouraged.

Quickly conversation moved on and the girls broke off into smaller, independent conversations. I was still confused as to whether Nicholas did actually live outside of Epping or if that had been a ploy to cover up that he lived in the Other World. Maybe he lived in Other Epping? I realised that I'd never actually asked where about he lived, I'd just assumed that he lived in Other London as he was spent so much time in Real London, and he seemed familiar with the Other City. But it could be that he just visited often, and actually resided somewhere much nicer. I'll have to ask him later on, I thought.

Come the end of the night Nicholas offered to walk me home. It was a welcome offer, as my friends had all dispersed. Bronagh had decided to go on to a club, of course, with another group of people she knew in the pub, along with Becks. Susie and Stacey lived in Dormitory's slightly set apart from ours, so were venturing a different way, and I didn't really want to walk back that late on my own. We left the pub hand in hand, after saying our drunken exaggerated good-byes for 10 minutes, and almost instantly the mix of alcohol and fresh air left me feeling giddy.

'You were amazing tonight!' I declared, glancing side wards at Nicholas.

'Was I?' He asked, seemingly surprised.

'Yes, you were! You totally won them over!' I smiled and squeezed his hand with pride.

'I wasn't sure that I would manage it with Bronagh, she seems like she could be a tough old cookie!' He laughed.

'She is. But she took to you!' I eyed him coyly, 'Did you put thoughts in her mind?' I asked him in mock accusation.

'I would never!' He held his hands up but chuckled to himself.

I breathed in quickly, in mock horror.

'No, I didn't,' He told me more seriously, 'It would have been fun to though.'

'Mmmm.' I gave him a dig.

'So, Gemma, can I ask you a question?'

'I think you just did.' I teased.

'What are we?' he asked more seriously.

'What do you mean?'

'Like to each other. At the risk of sounding corny, are we boyfriend and girlfriend now?'

'Do you want to be?' I asked, hope and nerves suddenly circulating inside of me.

'Yes, of course I do.' He turned and kissed me hard before continuing, 'If you do?'

I kissed him back, running my fingers through his hair and pulling him down further to me so I could kiss him more urgently. I felt a stirring inside me that I had never felt before and I knew right then, with no more words being needed,

Nicholas and I were now an item. I also knew, he wouldn't be going home tonight.

The next morning, I awoke to find myself wrapped tightly within Nicholas arms. He was gently snoring, so I knew he was still asleep, and I allowed myself some time to savour the moment. I'd never felt contentment like this before and it felt good. I twisted slightly to allow myself to watch Nicholas for a while, but I knew if I turned too much chances were, I would wake him up. So, I inched my body slightly and then craned my neck as far as I could, so I was able to just about see him out of the corner of my eye. I lay watching him for several minutes. Suddenly Nicholas' eyes popped open and he looked at me rather bemusedly.

'Er, what are you doing?' He asked.

'I wanted to watch you, but if I moved my body too much, I'd have woken you up!' I explained.

'So, you just risked breaking your neck instead?' He chuckled.

I rolled completely over so we were face to face.

'That's how much I wanted to watch you sleep, Boyfriend.' I grinned hard.

'Huh? Boyfriend?' He feigned confusion.

'Ah well if you've forgotten then I suppose I better get going and move on to the next!' I joked, edging slowly out of bed.

'Come here.' He grabbed my hand and pulled me back to him.

He wrapped his arms around me once more, 'Of course I've

not forgotten, Girlfriend!'

We kissed slowly, with less urgency and more softness than the night before. It was the most magical thing to happen to me, since I'd discovered actual magic.

'Gemma, are you ready to go?!' Bronagh stormed in looking mildly annoyed, followed by mildly surprised, 'I'm so sorry, I didn't realise you had company – I'll just be, I'll be going…'

Nicholas and I both laughed as the door slammed shut.

'I've never seen her lost for words before!' I giggled.

'Well I don't think she'll be walking in on you without knocking again!' Nicholas smirked.

We heaved ourselves out of bed and I quickly covered myself with a light dressing gown. I might have been confident enough to whip my clothes off in the drunken darkness last night, but I was feeling more conscious of my lumps and bumps in the cold light of day and wasn't ready for anyone to see me naked in the unforgiving daylight. Nicholas didn't seem to notice, instead searching the mounds of clothes on the floor looking for anything that belonged to him. He has such a good body, I admired, maybe I should consider joining a gym too? Or eating a little healthier?

'I love your body just as it is!' Nicholas proclaimed, and then flushed the brightest red I'd seen anyone go.

In return, I too flushed red.

'I'm so sorry!' Nicholas declared, 'I didn't mean to – honestly! I heard it as clear as if you were speaking to me, I would never have replied if I'd known. Oh god, I feel awful! I would never invade your private thoughts on purpose…'

'It's ok Nicholas,' I interrupted him, 'I promise! I know you didn't mean to!'

It was my turn to wrap my arms around him, he was clearly mortified, and I wanted to offer him some comfort.

'I don't even know why it's happening Gemma; I've never heard anyone's private thoughts like this before.'

'I'm sure there's a simple reason.' I tried to find explanation, but I couldn't.

'I'm going to seek some advice. After it happened in the park, and now this, it wouldn't be right if I didn't try to find some control on it – I promise you I will try to make it stop.'

'It's ok, don't worry. Just don't use it against me in an argument!' I winked.

'I won't, I promise.' Nicholas sighed, almost relieved to be off the hook a little.

'Anyway, it's quite nice to know that you like my body the way it is, without me having to tell you I'm embarrassed of it!'

'It is the sexiest body I've ever seen!' He winked at me and made an animal type growl.

'Right, now you're just being creepy,' I laughed, 'And making me late. Off you pop, text you later!'

And with that I quickly kissed him and then ran out to the communal bathroom to get showered.

22 NEW APARTMENT

We found a place to live easier than I thought we would. Bronagh took charge, of course, and we spent a weekend visiting them all. Bronagh's sister dropped out of the viewings. Apparently, she had decided she didn't need to be in London for another couple of weeks. She spun Bronagh a tale about her work being delayed, but she did let slip to Bronagh that her ex was around, and I had a feeling that was the real reason she was delaying coming to London. None the less she paid her share of the deposit and first 3 months' rent so we made sure to find somewhere large enough to house all of us, as Becks had decided she was now going to be house sharing with some other friends so we no longer needed to account for her. It turns out it was quite an interesting thing to do, finding a place to live in London, and not interesting in a good way. The first place we visited described itself as a 3 bed exclusive let, but what it didn't mention was that the 3 bedrooms were actually split down from 1 large bedroom, and they each housed a single bed only – the rooms couldn't fit anything else in, literally. The single beds touched a wall either side. There was no space for a dresser or wardrobe, nor were there any windows. We politely told the man we'd get back to him, but as soon as we'd rounded the corner, we discredited that one. The next place we visited looked fairly promising. It was a share in an old Georgian house, which was typical for cheap London accommodation. Landlords took huge houses and split them up into house shares, with a bathroom or two, a communal living room and kitchen and as many bedrooms as they could feasibly house. It was on a leafy suburb street and I was genuinely excited by it. If we had the right housemates, it would be a great option for us. I hoped there would be other students, or young professionals for us to make friends with. We entered through the modern wooden door that stood in the middle of the double bay fronted house and were greeted by a beautifully restored, traditionally tiled entrance hall. It was wide and housed a large, open staircase that snaked around the side and back of the house, above which stood a huge great window that flooded the area with light. Bronagh and I looked at each other in surprise and delight. But, almost immediately as our host began to speak, I had an uncomfortable feeling overcome me. Our host gave us a thorough tour of his stunning house, but with every word he spoke I disliked him more and more. I didn't know why, it wasn't anything he said particularly, just his whole persona set my senses alight with displeasure. Bronagh, on the other hand, was struggling to hide her delight and almost squealed with excitement when the landlord showed us the 3 bedrooms that were on offer. They were all enormous, with King size beds and en-suites. Bronagh was pretty much ready to sign on the dotted line right there and then, but something told me I needed to probe a little further.

'Who are the other tenants?' I asked curiously.

The landlord hadn't mentioned any others, but there were clearly several more bedrooms than those he had showed to us, and I was unsure why he hadn't discussed who else lived there as it was usually normal practice.

'No other tenants.'

He looked me dead in the eye and I immediately felt like he was looking right through my clothes and seeing my naked body. I recoiled slightly, just as he gave a slight lick of his lips.

'I thought the ad said this was a house share?' I pushed on.

Bronagh shot me a death stare, in warning to stop asking questions, but I needed to probe further to understand the situation.

'It is, in a way…' He started to explain, 'I live here too.'

'That's no problem.' Bronagh broke in, 'Is it Gemma?'

'I'm not sure if we've got the price confused, as I thought I'd read that it was the same price as other places we've seen that are much smaller and, without being rude to them, nowhere near to this standard of accommodation?!' I persisted.

'The price is correct… I'm not so much concerned with the price as the er…' He wavered, '..the company.'

'The company?' I was momentarily confused.

'That's absolutely fine,' Bronagh went on, 'We completely understand that you wouldn't want to house share with just anyone.'

Bronagh smiled brightly looking backwards and forwards, from me to him, silently willing us to agree.

'I, er, like to keep a certain kind of company…' Our host went on awkwardly, 'In exchange for cheap, or free accommodation I get to be seen out with my tenants in public at regular intervals of my choosing.'

'Right…' Bronagh spoke slowly and more hesitantly, 'I'm sure that wouldn't be a problem, would it Gemma?'

'I may also require some small physical contact from time to time, again at my choosing.' He went on.

I felt sick, and I looked at Bronagh with pleading eyes. Please don't say this is ok, please don't agree, I pleaded in my head. The screaming in my head seemed to work, realisation suddenly seemed to dawn on Bronagh and her face recoiled in horror.

'You want what?! What are you, some kind of pervert? How dare you try to encourage vulnerable women into this sick situation. You do know that this would be classed as a type of prostitution?! You ought to be locked up, you dirty old git. Come on Gemma, we're going!' And with that Bronagh grabbed my hand and stormed us both out and almost dragged me all the way to our next destination.

The next place wasn't quite so terrifying, although it did seem to have an array of rats inhabiting the garden – and no doubt other places that we hadn't yet seen. The place after that was ok just quite far out, and the one after that again had bedrooms that resembled closets. I was starting to feel a little disheartened, and Bronagh was definitely losing interest fast, but I knew we needed to persevere, that something better was coming along.

As we walked up to what would eventually be our house share, I knew as soon as I looked at it that it would be the one. As we approached we could see it was a fairly small terraced house, but it was immaculately kept with a small picket fence surrounding the garden, and the flowers that lined it. The grass was healthy, and bright green. The window frames and door frames were perfectly painted in white, the same could not be said for many of the house shares we had viewed where the exterior had mostly been left to rot, and they framed the house perfectly. I looked to Bronagh and smiled.

'Don't get your hopes up!' She almost scolded me, but it was too late – I already had.

We knocked gently on the small knocker and a little, old couple answered the door.

'Good afternoon ladies, please come on in.' The woman gently instructed us and ushered us straight into the small living room. We all sat on the Sofa's and the couple offered us tea.

'Ooh yes please.' I nodded in delight.

'That's very kind, thank you.' Bronagh politely accepted.

As the old man pottered in the kitchen, making the tea, the old lady introduced herself.

'I'm Ethel,' She warmly shook our hands, 'And my husband is Gerald'.

'Gemma.' I replied.

'Bronagh.'

The man rattled through the door with a large tray holding a large teapot and a few teacups along with milk and sugar on the side.

'I'm Gerald.' He told us.

'I've told them dear. This is Gemma, and this is Bronagh.' Ethel introduced us to her husband.

'Pleasure to meet you.' He smiled broadly.

'You too!' We both chirped.

They both gently poured the tea and milk into the cups, after we'd advised we both took milk and no sugar, and passed our cups to us. The tea was a welcome relief to the fizzy drinks I'd grabbed all day being on the go, and I sat back feeling relaxed in the company.

'So, ladies, you're looking for somewhere to live?' Gerald started.

'Yes, we are at University here and they only allow first year students to live in the Dorms.' I explained.

'We also want to stay in the City through the Summer as we have part-time jobs.' Bronagh added.

'Ah, I see. We don't usually accept students…' Ethel started, and my heart began to sink, 'But we liked your application so we wanted to meet you.'

'Is there a third person?' Gerald asked.

'Yes, my sister,' Bronagh responded, 'But she travels with her work and she's not in the area at the moment. She will pay to keep her room for her though.'

'Ah I see, no problem.' Gerald continued.

'Well I suppose you want to know a little bit about us…' Ethel picked up, 'We've lived here for 60 years. We raised our children here, and we love this house. But when we both retired, we found it a bit too much for us. Gerald has problems with his joints, you see, and I just get tired very easily. So, we decided to rent some of the house out but, rather than just rent out some of the bedrooms, we got the house split into a type of apartments. That way we didn't have to share with strangers, and we could still live here, but we could get some extra money and have a smaller space to manage.'

'What a great idea.' I smiled from Ethel to Gerald.

'It's worked quite well for us ever since, but we are strict who we let move in mind.' She continued.

'Do you mind me asking why you usually refuse students?' Bronagh bravely ventured.

'Ah!' Gerald took over, 'We just don't want; how would you describe it… party animals. We're too old to be woken by drunken laughing in the middle of the night, and complaints from the neighbours.'

'Not that we're fuddy duddy's!' Ethel interrupted, 'The last couple that lived here went out almost every weekend, but they tried to keep their noise to a minimum when they got home.'

'Well you won't get any trouble from us!' I promised.

'I can sense that about you.' Ethel commented and looked straight at me, almost like she was letting me know that she had magic senses too.

'Let's show you girls around then.' Gerald stood and invited us to follow him.

We walked back outside and around to the side of the house where another door sat. As Gerald opened it, I could see there was a small space with a shoe rack and coat rail, and then a flight of stairs. Gerald sprang up the stairs a lot quicker than I imagined he would and as we reached the top he turned and winked and informed me he's a keen mountain climber. I smiled, I liked it here and felt at home before I'd even seen the rooms. We wondered around and observed a very pleasant living accommodation. The rooms were quite plain, creams and beiges all around, but were perfectly kept. The bedrooms were small and neat, but each housed a double bed and a small wardrobe with full length mirror hanging on the walls. The living room was open plan with a modern but small kitchen, and the bathroom missed a bath but had a nice sized shower unit. I was ready to move in there and then, and from the look on Bronagh's face I could tell she wanted it too.

'When are you shortlisting the applicants?' Bronagh asked.

'Ah, we don't do that as such.' Ethel explained.

'You see, we do that before we invite people to view, kind of.' Gerald continued.

'As much as we can…' Ethel went on, 'We get a feeling of people from their applications, then we invite them to view based on how much we like the feel of them.'

Again, Ethel looked straight at me.

'Well that sounds like as good a plan as any.' I nodded and smiled genuinely.

'It's never failed us yet!' Gerald smiled.

'Obviously if they came and we didn't get a good feeling from them in person then we wouldn't let them have the place, but it hasn't happened yet.' Ethel told us, as they both grinned to each other with pride.

'So, if you want it girls, it's yours.' Gerald announced cheerily, 'I understand you probably need time to think it over and finish your viewings…'

'We'll take it!' Bronagh practically jumped on them and immediately started shaking their hands.

I laughed at this typical Bronagh reaction, taking charge and jumping in at the deep end – but I couldn't be happier. I desperately wanted to live here and find out a bit more about Ethel and Gerald. I got the impression that I might have a fair bit in common with them.

Once we'd gone back downstairs and signed all of the paperwork and had another cup of tea with Ethel and Gerald, I'd made up my mind that they were definitely also of Magical ability. As Ethel had passed me the pen to sign the tenancy agreement a spark of electricity ignited as our hands brushed and we both looked at each other, partly in surprise and partly in a 'I know what you know' way. Gerald obviously sensed it too, as he stopped mid-sentence and looked from Ethel to me and back to Ethel. By the time Bronagh and I left I felt a comfortableness with Ethel and Gerald that I had never felt with people I'd just met before, and I knew I could relax here. Perhaps I might even learn a thing or two. I definitely needed to speak with Martha or Nicholas to find out how I could broach the subject with my new housemates, as I didn't want to get in to trouble. Maybe they'd even bring it up with me. I was excited to learn more about them and make some more 'magical' friends.

As we walked back to the tube station Bronagh was alighted

with excitement that we'd found somewhere to live, and that we didn't have to visit any more weird and wonderful places. She was animatedly talking about all the different features of our new home that she loved, but I wasn't really listening to her. Of course, I smiled and nodded along, agreeing with everything she said, but I was lost in my own thoughts and buzz and couldn't find focus for Bronagh.

'And it was all down to you, Gemma!' She announced loudly, smiling broadly at me and immediately cutting through my thoughts.

'What?' I questioned.

'This, our new home!' Bronagh declared, 'It was all down to you that we found it!'

'It was?' I had no idea what she was talking about.

'Yeah – the ad that you circled and pushed under my door for me to look at. Remember? A couple of nights ago. I mean, I wasn't sure when I first read it but I thought I'd add it on to the end of the day viewings, if we could fit it in, but my gosh it's the best thing I've ever done. Well done you, you deserve a drink – on me!'

'I did? I'm not sure… what made you think it was me? I don't even remember getting the paper.'

'Well the front had your name across the top, so I assumed you'd ordered a subscription for it. And what luck you chose that paper, as it was the only one I didn't buy, and the ad definitely wasn't in any of the others. It's just so lucky!'

'Or magic?' I muttered quietly, instantly realising that it must be the work of something more.

'Yes, maybe magic. Whatever you want to believe.'

Bronagh eyed me curiously, and I rolled my eyes and smiled as if I were joking. I might be thrilled with my newfound forces, and desperate to tell Bronagh all about it, but I wouldn't risk losing it by saying anymore.

23 LEARNING

We moved in quickly and easily. Neither Bronagh or I had much stuff, and her sister was still delayed. So, on the Saturday after we'd signed we arranged for a man with a van to come and load all of our belongings, hoist them across town and then unload for us. It took us less than an hour to unpack and tidy up our new home, and for our first Saturday evening we invited Ethel and Gerald upstairs with us for dinner and to watch some Saturday night dancing show that was extremely popular. We had a wonderful evening, and after that we started to often join Ethel and Gerald for a cup of tea when we were passing or invite them up to ours. To the naked eye we were an odd match of friendship, but it worked extremely well, and we were all pleased with our new living companions.

Exams had also finished for the Summer, and so Bronagh and I both upped our shifts in our respective jobs, which meant we inevitably saw each other less frequently whilst we worked hard to build up another nest egg of money ready for the start of next term. When I wasn't working, I was studying hard about my magical abilities, and magic in general. I was keen to learn all I could, and the more I learned the more I wanted to know. I had an insatiable thirst for all things to do with our senses and the Other World, I would spend a lot of time studying books and visiting the Other World alone to practice and observe.

One morning I awoke, ready for another shift in the coffee shop, and I instantly felt a crazy and disturbing mix of emotions. I had excitement fizzing through me, at the same time I couldn't keep the tears from my eyes. As I stood to walk to the bathroom I was overcome with fear and sat down on my bed, then I started hysterically laughing at absolutely nothing. I knew that something strange was going on, I felt like I was on a fairground ride of emotions, and it was disturbing. I picked up my phone and called Martha. After several rings she answered.

'Hello, Martha speaking, how may I help you?' Her voice chirped.

'Martha, it's me Gemma.' I tried to hide the nervousness from my voice.

'Gemma, is everything ok? You sound a little strange!' Martha's voice now mimicked the nerves I was feeling.

'I'm fine, it's just something strange is happening to me. Can I come over?'

'Of course. I have an appointment, but I'll call sick. Come straight over.'

I hung up and pulled on some clothes. I needed to get out of the apartment without running in to anyone, especially Bronagh, and the less time I spent wondering around trying to shower and eat, the better. I peeked my head around my bedroom door just in time for a surge of anger to hit me full force. I stormed down the hall and slammed the front door behind me. I banged all the way down the street and stormed on to Martha's. The adrenaline of being so angry made me feel full of energy, and I knew I needed to burn some of it off before I got to Martha's, I didn't want to frighten her. I walked and walked, but before I had realised it, I had rounded the corner to Martha's street. I had no idea we lived this close by, I must walk more often I thought to myself, yet as I did, I suddenly felt extremely upset again and begun crying and shaking. I ran to Martha's and knocked hard on her front door – I didn't want to alarm her, but I needed her to get to me before a well-meaning stranger passed by and tried to help. The door opened before I had even finished with the knocker, and Martha quickly ushered me inside.

'My dear girl, whatever is the matter? It's not that Everly girl is it? Or has something happened to your Mammy?' Martha was desperately trying to search for a reason, I knew I had to try to explain quickly.

'No, nothing like that – I just don't know what is happening to me. I woke up this morning and I have all of these crazy emotions running through me!' I told her.

'What kind of emotions?' Martha looked at me with interest.

'All kinds, literally every emotion under the sun has become of me this morning. I don't know what to do!'

'Are they quite extreme, and changing frequently?' Martha asked.

'Yes.' I answered her, just as I stopped crying and started laughing again.

'What have you been doing the last few days?'

'Working mostly, why?' I laughed uncontrollably.

'Ah Gemma, have you been working on your feeling sense?'

'Yes, I found this wonderful book written by Granny, I've

been learning so much!'

'Oh, I told Elsie that book would only cause trouble!' Martha tutted and shook her head.

'Trouble how? It's so informative!'

'Yes, I agree – it is so easy to follow and learn from. It is truly a gem. But what it fails to do is inform people that before you encourage your feeling sense you must first protect yourself.'

'Protect yourself from what?'

'Opening yourself up as a floodgate for everyone else's emotions. That's what has happened to you Gemma, you've been trying to enhance your sense, which is wonderful, but you didn't know to protect yourself first. And because you've been working you've spent a lot of time with the public and lots of people who all have different emotions at the moment – what you are experiencing now is all of them!'

'I am?' I was momentarily stunned out of feeling anything. But then like someone had turned a light switch on they were back, and I was suddenly very restless and agitated.

'Right, I'll get my coat.' Martha told me.

'Where are we going?' I barked, and then hung my head sheepishly, 'Sorry!'

'We're going to see Malachy, see if we can stop this.'

Malachy was already waiting for us when we arrived. He was stood in the fabulous entrance hall, which looked even more fabulous than usual. There were no warm welcomes this time though, just a beckoning as he strode past us at speed.

'Come with me, ladies.' He instructed us.

We followed Malachy out into the garden again, but rather than sitting in his usual spot at the table and chairs we proceeded to walk down the lawn, over a small bridge sitting across a stream, and into a tall tree lined space. There was ivy covering all of the walls that surrounded the lawn, and the stream ran across the bottom, with a small waterfall filling the space with relaxing sounds. In the middle of the lawn sat two large beanbag style seats and a pink yoga mat. Malachy ushered us over and gestured for Martha to take a seat on one of the beanbags, and I to take the yoga mat. He sat down on the beanbag and paused quietly for a couple of minutes before speaking.

'Gemma, Martha... Welcome.'

'Thank you for seeing us.' Martha nodded to him.

'Now Gemma, it seems that you have a very sensitive sense to those feelings of others.'

I nodded without looking up, I was lay flat on my back staring at the sky and willing to get off this rollercoaster.

'Unfortunately, it is difficult to reverse this, so the best we can do is stay calm and keep you away from others of no magic until this fades out. Then we can run a protection spell, to minimise the effect of this again.'

'Ok, so what do we do now?' I almost whispered, fear running through me.

'Well this is our Zen garden, welcome. I will talk you through a type of meditation to relax you, and I will also offer you a potion at the end that will act as a form of sedative and hopefully put you to sleep for a while. That should see you through the worst phase. Once you are awake again, I will assess you and create a plan from there.'

'But if I can't be around those from the Real world where will I go to sleep?'

'Don't worry about that!' Martha interjected, 'We will try to get you back to mine.'

'For now, Gemma, I need you to take some deep breaths, relax and focus on the sounds around you rather than the noise of the feelings.'

I lay back and tried to ignore the struggle of my internal feelings. I listened to Malachy's gentle chanting, I listened to the water steadily running around the perimeter, and I listened to the gentle breeze rustling through the leaves. The whole setting was very relaxing, and I could completely understand why it was being used as a Zen Garden. It was delightful. Just being here made me feel a lot less worried, and a calmness started to come over me. I wanted a Zen Garden, I thought. Perhaps not a full garden, but a Zen space. I'll have to get some tips from Malachy and look into it when this is over. That would be lovely, a calming space I could go to where I could relax my body and thoughts. I'm sure it would help with my studies as well as my magic sense, I thought. I would definitely investigate it later in the week. I wonder if I could use this Zen Garden, I thought. Is it open to the public? It can't be. Otherwise people would be coming and going all the time and it wouldn't be very Zen. I'd have to remember to ask if there were anywhere like this I could use though. Malachy would know.

As I lay still and let my mind wonder I felt my emotions start to settle, as my brain started to focus on other things. I wondered if I should let Malachy know.

'Keep breathing deeply and staying very still and quiet Gemma.' He instructed, mid chant.

I bet Malachy is another of those that can read minds, I speculated.

'Block out your own thoughts Gemma and focus on the sounds and sensations surrounding you.' Malachy advised me, and I fought really hard to block out everything internally and focus on the external.

I didn't remember falling asleep, or being given any kind of potion, but I must have because I woke up and looked around and had absolutely no idea where I was. The mixture of feelings running through me was less so now, and the intensity was much less severe so the effect on me was only a little disturbing. I was able to focus on where I was, and I sat up in the bed that I had been sleeping in and looked around. This wasn't Martha's house; I was sure of it. For a start the bedding was very modern, and not at all to Martha's tastes. The window in the room was also out of sorts to be Martha's house, it was a tiny single glazed sash window with lead pattern running through it and looked more fitting as part of an extremely old country cottage. I stood up and looked out of the window to see what was outside and I noticed that the surround of the window was covered in leaves, which made me think the house had some ivy growing around the walls. The garden was barely visible due to a wooden type structure covered in plantation blocking the view, but I could see beyond the garden was meadows upon meadows. I definitely wasn't at Martha's, nor was I at the Visitor Centre. As I turned to face the door, I could hear some footsteps in the corridor, and I felt curious as to who was behind it. I trusted Malachy and Martha with my life, so I knew wherever I was I would be safe and come to no harm, but I couldn't for the life of me figure out where I might be. As the footsteps neared to the room they slowed down, until they stopped outside the door. Clearly the person on the other side was hesitating to see if they could hear me awake, and I was feeling a bit too nervous to open the door, so I gently called out instead.

'Erm, Hello?' I muttered.

The door instantly swung open and a beaming Nicholas filled the doorway.

'Oh, thank goodness!' I declared as I flew to him and wrapped my arms tightly around him, burying my face in his chest.

'I'm glad to see you awake and ok!' Nicholas looked down at me, pulling my face out and tilting it to his.

'I'm glad I'm not in a house with some randomers!' I told him.

'Ha!' He laughed, 'Well I suppose that depends on what you'd class as a randomer!'

'Well yes, I suppose you are a bit weird.' I teased.

'I'll take that as a compliment!' He winked, 'Come on, there's tea freshly brewed downstairs.'

Nicholas led me down a very narrow and steep stairway to a large living space with a huge open fire. We walked straight through the living room and into a typical old kitchen, with cobbled tile like flooring, a huge farmhouse type table and an Aga brewing some tea in the corner. Very traditional, very not what I expected from Nicholas.

'Is this your house?' I asked.

'Yes – well it was my parents, and I've stayed here. Lots of memories and love, I couldn't bare to leave.'

'It's beautiful.'

'Yes, it is lovely. Probably not as contemporary and state-of-the-art as I'd like, but it has its own charm.'

'It is quite like my parents' house actually, only older.' I informed him whilst looking around.

'Oh really? You'll feel comfortable here then!' He smiled.

'How did I end up here?' I asked, suddenly very curious.

'Martha called me and asked if you could come here. Apparently, they were going to walk you to Martha's house when you were a bit calmer and had some potion, but you fell asleep instantly. So, they had to levitate you somewhere, which obviously couldn't be in the Real World, so they called me.'

'And you came to my rescue.' I cooed.

'Well obviously I wanted to say No, it could affect my image as a bit of a player around here, but I can't resist a Damsel in distress.... And Martha is an endearing damsel!' He laughed aloud.

'Oh, very funny!' I giggled, 'So how long have I been asleep?'

'About 26 hours.'

'No, really?'

'Yes really. I think they said you got to the Visitor Centre just before 10 in the morning yesterday, it is midday now.'

'Oh my gosh, that's crazy!'

'Yes, but not unusual… How are you feeling now?' He kissed my head softly as he handed me my tea and joined me at the table.

'A bit better, I've still got some emotions running riot but there doesn't seem to be as many and it's not as intense as yesterday.'

'Oh Gemma, I'm so sorry, I feel terrible about this. And so does Martha. Neither of us even gave it a thought to tell you to use a protection spell. It's often the first thing that they teach, but obviously because you've been teaching yourself you didn't know. I should have engaged my brain when you said about the books from the store, but I was just so full of our date I didn't think. Sorry!' He hung his head.

'It's not your fault, honestly! Anyway, it's a learning curve for me. Scary, but at least I know my senses are strong, and the studying I'm putting in is paying off.'

'Absolutely.' Nicholas nodded.

'And I got to see where you live out of it too.' I winked.

'Ah so that was your cunning plan!' He smirked, 'You know you could have just asked.'

'I've never liked doing things the easy way.' I grinned back.

'Hmmm, I can imagine. Right, well if you're feeling up to it, I'll give you the grand tour?'

Nicholas showed me around his stunning home. I was right about the Ivy, it completely covered the whole house with the exception of the windows and doors, it was a magnificent sight. The garden was surrounded by a cobbled brick wall, and a small path ran from a gate to the front door. Around the back of the house was a kind of sanctuary. There were wooden beams overhead, which must have formed part of the wooden structure I looked down on from the bedroom, with foliage wrapped all around it. Lights hung at various levels from the beams, and there were large cushions dotted all around, with various statues in and amongst them. It felt almost as Zen as the Visitor Centre Zen Garden, and it was exactly the kind of thing I'd been dreaming of when I was lay daydreaming with Malachy and Martha.

'This is amazing!' I told Nicholas.

'I like privacy, and I wanted to create a place I could relax in.' He explained.

'Well this is perfect for that; can we spend some time out here today?' I asked him.

'Of course, I've done us some lunch, so I'll just go and fetch it out. Sit where you like.'

'Thank you… Nicholas?'

'Yes.'

'Is it ok for me to stay here whilst this is still passing?'

Nicholas came back out with a tray and placed it down in front of us as he sat next to me.

'Of course it is, I wouldn't want you to be anywhere else!'

24 THE OTHER WORLD

We spent the whole of the first day and evening in Nicholas garden. We lounged around during the day. We chatted, read books, listened to the radio. Nicholas' garden was even more perfect by night, with string lights all around creating a peaceful atmosphere. It was perfect, and I wondered why I didn't take more time off to relax like this. I also enjoyed having someone take care of me, cooking my meals and making my drinks. But by the next morning I was starting to feel a bit of cabin fever, and desperately wanted to get out and do something. Malachy visited me early to see how I was doing, but the feelings phenomena hadn't completely gone and so he insisted he needed to come back in order to assist with a protection spell. Despite this, he did deem me well enough to go out so long as we stayed in the Other World. Apparently, most people in the Other World would have their own protection magic, and this would be enough to keep me safe from their feelings. I was thrilled that I could explore some more of this wonderful place, and Nicholas even seemed happy that he had to take care of me for a little while longer. I'd text Bronagh and told her that I'd fallen ill while with Nicholas, and wouldn't be home until I was better, so I was free to spend time here without having to face any difficult questioning.

'What do you want to do today then?' Nicholas asked me, as he laid down a freshly brewed pot of tea at the Kitchen table.

'I'm not sure… what do you want to do?' I asked him.

'I don't know. We could go for a walk? Or go to the cinema?'

He suggested.

'Well actually, I wanted to ask you about this place I've been reading about?' I told him.

'What place would that be?' He eyed me curiously.

'It's a Woods called Ever After, have you heard of it?'

'Yes, I have.' Nicholas looked away.

'Have you been?' I persisted gently.

'I have. But look Gemma, it's not the place for you just now.'

'But I've heard it's where people of magic go when they pass away, where the spirits can live on and I'd really like to talk to my Granny – and I think she could help me with this…'

'I know Gemma, but it's not really that safe.'

'It's not? But I thought people that lived in the Other World are good, that the magic is regulated for good deeds?'

'It is, mostly. However, like with anything, there are magical geniuses that do figure out how to break the boundaries and use magic for bad. A bit like computer hackers, it is very difficult to do, and they often get caught very quickly, but some extremely intelligent Others do get away with bad acts. Unfortunately, it is those with the bad intentions that often want to live on, and cause trouble, so many of them also inhabit the woods. Don't get me wrong, there are also many good souls there too, but you need to know how to navigate it. Plus, in your vulnerable state it wouldn't be a good idea to go there today. Let's talk about it again in a few months.'

I was disheartened, I'd pinned my hopes on getting to speak with Granny soon, but what Nicholas had said made perfect sense, it also explained why Mammy and Martha had never mentioned it to me. And I didn't want to risk myself getting infected with any more crazy feelings.

'I know, how about we take a ride out to the Old Town? There's the Magical History museum we could visit, and you could learn more about Magic, the people and The Other World?'

'Oh yes Nicholas, that sounds fantastic! I've never heard of it, but it sounds fantastic – just what I'm interested in!'

'And there's a cracker of a pub not far from the museum, that sits on the water and sells good pub grub and beer – we could go there when we've finished exploring for something to eat and drink!' Nicholas looked rather pleased with himself for this idea, and I smiled at him.

'That sounds like the best plan I've heard all day!'

We had a late morning brunch before we left and headed out into the Midday sun. Nicholas directed me down the country lane that ran in front of his house, and we walked for approximately 10 minutes before I could see an intersection in front of us. The street that he lived on was typical of the countryside, with no road markings and plenty of loose stones. There were few buildings dotted along the side, but it was mostly fields and a peaceful calmness stilled in the air. It was much quieter than even my hometown, on this street, and I wondered how far we actually were from the Other City Centre. However, as we approached the end, I could see a somewhat busier street, and could hear a bell jangling.

Nicholas told me we needed to hurry so we picked up the pace and hurried to the main street. I followed Nicholas to a strange bus stop type of thing, and as I looked around, I saw the cause of the bell noise.

'A tram?!' I turned to Nicholas as a baffled look took over my face, and he laughed in response.

'Yes, a tram.' He confirmed to me, nodding.

'But… Why? How?'

'They take their purpose very seriously in the old town. Nothing gets in or out unless it's on something old fashioned!'

'No way! That is amazing!'

An old-style double decker tram pulled up to us and I wondered at it in awe. It was a stunning sight and instantly I was even more pleased with Nicholas' suggestion of a day out to the Old Town.

'I love old things.' I told him, without being asked.

'Most people of magic do. They understand them better. We are able to read their history with our minds, and it makes them so much more interesting.'

'I didn't know that, that's so fascinating!'

As we jumped on to the Tram the conductor punched into 2 tickets and gave them to Nicholas in exchange for the fare. We headed upstairs to find it was open topped and took a seat near the front.

'When the trams were invented, they had many problems,

mostly the smell and pollution, but also they toppled over and derailed frequently. In the Other World they quickly figured out how to overcome these issues with some magical help, but the Real World just moved on from them and invented a newer form of public transport. But here the elders of the old town were quite partial to the Tram system, and felt it was a waste to just be rid of them, so they insisted they stay as the transport link to the town. To this day nothing more modern has passed the boundaries, the only way in is by Tram or foot.'

'That is incredible, to have gone this long and still stood defiant against more modern transport! Good for them! How do you know all of this?'

'I used to come here a lot as a small boy. My Nan and Grandad were fond of the place, so they used to bring me, and we'd walk along the River and have chips in newspaper.'

'Ah, that sounds like it was good times.'

'The best!' He smiled at me, and continued to smile at the memories even as he turned away.

The journey was short and pleasant. It was almost like watching the transformation of the world back to times gone by. The buildings lining the streets slowly evolved from modern and sleek to smaller and full of character. I could see from Nicholas' face that he was excited to be back here, and the feeling inside of me matched him, I couldn't wait to get out and explore.

Although there was no fencing or gates, there was a very obvious border surrounding the old town. Even the pavement instantly changed once you'd entered, and the tram juddered along the cobbled ground, almost immediately coming to a stop once we were safely within the old town boundaries. We disembarked and I stood for a moment looking around all angles, taking in the wonder before me.

'So, when exactly does this date back to?' I asked Nicholas.

'It's hard to say.' Nicholas advised, 'You see, some of the buildings were here before others. The pub and the chip shop were amongst the first, the church is much older still. Some of the houses were built around the 1920's I think, but some of the living accommodation got rebuilt to create a more modern environment. That was about the 1940's. That was how this whole place became the old town really, the residents hated the new buildings, my Nan would describe them as monstrous and most of the elders felt the same way. So, the residents decided they would fight as hard as they could against any changes to their town. It was almost a revolt against the council, and so things went unchanged from then on, due to the fight from the people – it wasn't worth the effort from the powers that be.'

'Gosh! And now?' I queried.

'It's protected now. But even if it weren't, it's such a tourist area that I think there would be huge uproar if they were to try to modernise it.'

'Good, we need more places like this to preserve our history!'

'Indeed, we do. Shall we head straight to the museum?' Nicholas asked.

'That sounds great!'

The museum was a short walk away and sat on the bank of the

River. It was an old, disused factory that locals had used to store old artefacts that had value or sentimental value, our guide told us. The residents were keen to preserve the most interesting items that they had, or that they'd been left by older relatives, and it soon became apparent that others wanted to also enjoy viewing these items, and so the museum was born. Over time it had grown and now it was open to all, not just the residents, and the money it generated was put back into the upkeep of the town. Within the museum we saw old versions of a wand, which were much larger and not as discrete as the wands I'd seen in the bookstore. There was also a huge book of spells. Our guide explained that when the book first came about very few people could read and write, it was only the most elite. However, the community leaders had an idea of recording spells that were like recipe's in the Real World, passed down through generations, so that they never got lost in times gone by and could be utilised for many years to come. So, an educated person from each town was appointed to take down the details of the most powerful and precious spells and write them out on to pieces of paper. These were then added to the book, if they were deemed important enough, and the book is still used as a referral in modern day magic research. It stood behind a glass cabinet and it was the most exquisite leather-bound book, with perfect calligraphy to match the elegance of the pages. I longed to flick through it, but only authorised researchers and historians were allowed access these days, I was politely informed.

We moved on to another area which showed an array of wooden poles and small tree trunks. The guide explained to us that way back before transport existed one of the great teachers of magic had this idea that you could take an object and make it move by using the right spell. His inner circle all agreed that this should be possible, and they set about working out ways to make objects move. They did this easily with small items, but they struggled to make larger objects move in a cohesive manner over longer distances. Their idea was to make larger objects, that could bear the weight of heavy items such as people and items, that could assist with bringing water and food supplies to the home from a greater distance. One of them came up with the idea that tree logs would be good, as they were easily and cheaply available, and they could be made into any length to carry various sized loads. Plus, they would be easy to sit on. However, they found that; the larger the tree trunks, the harder it was to handle, and so the size started to be reduced as their experiments took shape. Eventually the trunks were quite thin, and resembled the broomstick handles that were used, and that is where the notion of witches riding on broomsticks came from. I was fascinated, and my mind was almost completely blown by this amazing explanation of common folklore.

Next, we came to a selection of large pots, and instantly I knew this was the history of the cauldron. Again, our guide explained that the villagers would often use large pots to boil water and cook food, so they were easily accessible and it was these that they would use when they needed to mix a lot of ingredients to make a spell. Very often each extended family would only have one pot between them, so it was usual for it to be exceptionally large. Things have changed now, we were told, and although some spells still require manual mixing many people have an array of utensils to choose from so the traditional pot, or cauldron, tends to only be used by the elders.

We continued to pass through many areas that talked about the history of magic, and I was surprised to learn that many of the women persecuted for witchcraft in the Witch trials were actually a type of herbalist that supplied herbal medicines. This was deemed to be witchcraft during the hysteria but was merely nothing more than the power of the utilisation of nature and its healing properties.

The last section that I found particularly interesting was the animals. As a child I'd always associated witches with black cats, and occasionally other small animals, and it turns out that animals do play a large part in those that live with magic. Cats are extremely popular as pets, and accomplices, in the Other World, due to their quick and agile abilities and their extreme intelligence. Colour is insignificant, explained our Guide. Whilst black cats are what popular preconception tells us are a witch's ally, this was only believed because of their ability to move around mostly unnoticed after dark, in the times when street lighting was uncommon. These days, any colour cat is fine. Lots of other small animals are also popular, especially those with intelligence and agility such as lizards in hotter climates and birds.

'Do you have an animal?' I asked Nicholas after we'd finished our tour of the museum and were stepping out of the exit.

'Yep, I have Wilfred.' He replied.

'How come I never saw Wilfred at the house?' I wondered.

'He lives outside, he's a Harvest Mouse.'

'Can I meet him later?'

'Sure. I'll see if he's around.'

We spent the remainder of the afternoon exploring the town and all the places that were used more as tourist attractions now. We visited the old, yet charming church, that opened its doors to tourists every day except for Sundays which was reserved solely for residents. We went to see the now defunct school, which consisted of 3 small classrooms and a hall. Nicholas told me that the local community of children grew too large for it as time went on, and so a larger school was built down the road, as the locals refused to allow any changes to be made to the original school, but it hadn't been used for anything since so now stood as another type of museum. We also visited the old shops, which were very much as I expected and a world away from the supermarkets of today. Each petite store had one small room with a counter, and each had their own specialty. There was a chemist, a greengrocer, a butcher and a traditional sweet shop. They still operated now, as they had done then, Nicholas told me, but the prices were high and so it was mostly the novelty effect which caused tourists to shop in them that kept them going. I too, as many other tourists did, felt compelled to make some purchases in there just to add to the trade and turnover to keep these wonderful historical shops open for generations to come. I purchased a small basket, like those that the original towns folk would have used to hold their shopping and were still woven by local women, and packed up the vegetables and meat I had purchased for dinner, and a small, fresh cake for afters. As we rounded the corner from the shops, having bought all we'd needed, Nicholas took the basket from me and promptly gave it a type of poem of instructions.

'Er, what was that?' I asked as the basket drifted off.

'Oh sorry!' Nicholas laughed, 'I forgot that you'd not yet seen this kind of magic.'

'That was amazing! Where has it gone?'

'It's gone home, it was a rhyming spell – they were very popular back in the day, and old school magic is still widely used and accepted in the Old towns.'

'Wow, what else do they do around here?' I questioned, desperate to see more.

'Well, lots of different things.' Nicholas looked around for inspiration.

'Look, see over there,' He pointed towards a small mid terraced house, 'They are cleaning their windows with the type of spells your mom uses for warming her towels, and no doubt cleaning her house.'

I looked over to where he was showing me and sure enough a woman was pointing and talking to a cleaning cloth that was rubbing the windowpanes clean all by itself.

'They might not be the sophisticated, modern magic of today, but they work perfectly well.' He advised me.

'So why doesn't everyone with magic use this to clean their windows?'

'We have spells that clean them instantly now, but a lot of the older community still prefer this method – they reckon the elbow grease brings up a more flawless clean.'

'Ha, that certainly sounds like something Mammy would say!' I chuckled.

'I don't know about you, but I'm starving!' Nicholas declared.

'Shall we go back and see if our food has made it home?' I asked, trying to hide my disappointment at having to leave.

'Ah that'll be fine for tomorrow, Wilfred will make sure it gets to the fridge. I thought we might grab a drink and eat at the pub I was telling you about? They do the best traditional home cooked food around! If you feel up to it?'

'Sounds perfect.' I smiled.

25 OLD TOWN EVENING

After we purchased our drinks, we headed into the garden and found a nice table on the edge of the River in the corner of the lawn. It was starting to become dusky and my stomach rumbled hard as the aroma of all the other diners meals passed by. I looked at the menu and was surprised to see very old school dishes listed.

'Something wrong?' Nicholas asked.

'No, not at all. I just wasn't expecting it to be quite so, erm what's the word… classical.'

Nicholas roared with laughter.

'Classical?!'

'Yeah!' I responded defiantly.

'That's a nice way to describe it!' He tried hard to stifle his laughter, but it hung on and infected me until I laughed too.

'I didn't want to say old!' I blushed.

'Is it ok for you?' He asked me more seriously.

'Yes, it makes a nice change!' I told him, 'Plus it reminds me of my Granny's cooking.'

Nicholas smiled and went back to perusing his menu. I looked up and down the list again and was delighted to see some of Granny' favourites on there. Cheese, Potato and Onion Pie was the first thing that caught my eye, I used to eat that all the time as a small child and just the thought of it brought back some wonderful memories of Granny's house. But then I came across Corned Beef Hash and my heart leapt. I loved Corned Beef Hash with a passion. It was one of those meals that I never thought to make for myself, but every time I had it, I wished I'd have it more. It was also the meal that Mammy would always ask for whenever we used to eat at Granny's altogether. I looked up at Nicholas to see if he had come to a decision, but he was still hunched over with a confused expression across his face.

'Tough choice?' I asked him.

'Yeah!' He answered without looking up, 'I'm torn between the Meat and Potato pie and the Bacon and Egg pie.'

'Ooh I've never heard of Bacon and Egg pie.' I shrugged.

'I've had them both here before, and they're both fantastic! But I'll go with the Bacon and Egg, so you can try a bit!'

'Ah you're too kind!' I winked at him.

'What are you having?' He asked as he stood to go and order.

'Corned Beef Hash please.'

'Great choice!' He declared nodding, before he wondered off inside to order.

I sat back and took in my surroundings. By now the sun was just about set and the sky was a stunning shade of grey / blue. There were hundreds of small twinkling lights dotted all around, that seemed to be shimmering in the air, and made for the most romantic setting. I felt a twang of uncertainty in my stomach and realised that I hadn't noticed the effect of other people's emotions all day, until now. I must be getting back to normal, I thought, but I wasn't yet ready to go back to the Real World and my real life. I was having such a wonderful time with Nicholas and learning all about the Other World that I wanted to stay for another day or two. As it turned out, Malachy was a certified Doctor, so he had issued me with a Doctor's note to get out of work for a week and so there was no hurry for me to go back on that front. Bronagh text me frequently to see how I was, but she didn't push for me to go home, I think she just genuinely wanted to ensure I was ok. I knew that she wouldn't mind me staying away for a small while longer. I just had to hope Malachy or Nicholas didn't realise I was ready to go back.

'I got you another drink.' Nicholas laid a small glass in front of me.

'What is it?' I asked, not recognising the light-coloured liquid.

'It's Mead, they brew it here so it's a must have!' Nicholas told me.

'That sounds great, thank you. This place is great Nicholas, I love it so much. It's got such a good vibe about it.'

'Yeah it's pretty cool isn't it! I love coming here.'

'Thank you so much for bringing me, I feel like I've learned so much too. That Magic Museum was so informative.'

'Ah I'm glad you thought so! I think, because most people I know have all been taught it for so long we take the knowledge for granted and assume everyone knows, so I kind of forget what to tell new people and what not to tell.'

'The history stuff is so interesting, I loved learning about how the preconceptions of witches came about – some of it is really quite amusing.'

'I agree. I hate the way some of the poor souls were treated, especially those that were hunted down, but I do smile at the way history has been twisted and the Real World believe they created the so-called 'Myths' of Witches.'

The waitress walked over with a couple of plates and placed them in front of us. Both meals looked fantastic and we instantly fell silent as we tucked into our dinner. As we sat quietly, I became aware of a dull buzzing noise around us and as my belly started to fill up, I slowed to ask Nicholas what the noise might be.

'Oh, that's just the fireflies.' He explained.

'Fireflies?'

'Yes – sorry I thought they'd mentioned this in the museum… Maybe we missed that bit! So back before electricity people would use magic to congregate fireflies in one space to create a light in the dark. They would use them to create light in places that might need it such as streets and public spaces.'

'That is so cool! Why did they stop using them?'

'Well as street lighting became more popular the need for the fireflies stopped, man-made light created a lot more light than fireflies ever could so it was one of the modern-day items that was quickly embraced.'

'But the fireflies are just so beautiful and romantic.' I quipped, staring up at the hundreds of them in the night sky.

'I suppose they are,' Nicholas smiled, 'Buggers to control when they get angry though!'

We continued to eat with very little conversation, and I got lost in the sound of the fireflies. Once we'd finished our main meals, we enjoyed some Bread and Butter pudding, and a few more drinks before merrily heading back to catch the last Tram. I smiled the whole journey back, as I enjoyed the fizz from the alcohol and the buzz from the feeling I got snuggled into Nicholas arms. I wasn't sure the evening could get any better, but then we got to Nicholas front garden.

'There he is.' Nicholas broke through my thoughts as we walked up the path.

'Huh, there who is?' I asked.

'Wilfred, look over there.' Nicholas pointed ahead, but I couldn't see anything.

'I don't see him, where?'

'Right over there, curled up asleep.' He pointed again, and my gaze followed his arm but all I could see was some flowers in a window box.

'I can't see him?!' I squinted and took a step closer, and that's when I noticed him, curled up inside a flower head as if it were his cocoon.

'See him now?' Nicholas asked.

'I do, that is the cutest thing!' I exclaimed.

'It's his usual hiding place. He likes the crops too, but the tulips are by far his favourite place to take a rest.' He chuckled.

'And that really has put a perfect end to the perfect day of discovering.' I smiled on the outside as well as on the inside.

The next morning, I woke up to find Nicholas dressed and talking quietly to Malachy in the Kitchen.

'Ah Gemma, you're awake.' Malachy greeted me.

'Hi Malachy, how are you?' I responded.

'I'm very good thank you. I heard you spent a long day learning yesterday?' He asked.

'Yes, it was amazing. I learnt so much, I loved it!'

'Oh good. And how are you feeling now?' He eyed me curiously.

'Slightly better…' I told him hesitantly.

'You were still a little restless in the night,' Nicholas joined in, 'I'm not sure she's fully better to return to normal just yet.'

'Hmmm…' Malachy eyed me curiously again, 'I can't sense anything, but I suppose another day's rest wouldn't hurt if you're not feeling completely back to normal. If that's ok with you Gemma?'

'Yes!' I answered quickly and they both looked at me in surprise at my eagerness, 'I mean, if you both think it's best.'

Nicholas turned away as he smirked to himself, and I nodded earnestly.

'Right then, I'll be back in the morning to give you some protection. Until then please do take it easy, it will help your body fight off anything that shouldn't be there.' Malachy instructed, as he faded into the air.

'How did he...?' I started to ask, but then remembered where I was and gave up wondering.

'Do you want some breakfast?' Nicholas asked, pulling some bread out of the wrapper and pushing it in to the toaster.

'Yes, please. And a cuppa!' I winked.

'Cheeky!' He grinned.

'Malachy said to rest!' I insisted, laughing at Nicholas eye roll.

'Yeah, yeah. Sit your bottom down then Madam, and I will serve you shortly.' He chuckled back at me.

'So, what are we going to do today?' I asked.

'Well Malachy is right; you should be resting. I didn't think yesterday would be quite so full on as it was, so I suggest maybe a Netflix and chill kind of day?' Nicholas looked at me out of the corner of his eye and flashed me a devilish grin.

'Sounds just what I need!' I agreed, and suddenly I was ready to get back to bed without breakfast.

Malachy returned the next day and performed a simple spell on me. It was stunning to watch Malachy at work, and it was clear from his confidence and ease with magic that he was a master in the field. He spoke softly but without pause as he chanted the spell, and then pulled out a small potion for me to drink. The smell was incredibly strong, and made my eyes water, but both Malachy and Nicholas gestured for me to go ahead. The taste was actually not that bad and reminded me of some sweets that I used to eat as a child that were made with aniseed. Following that Malachy taught me a protection spell for me to use on myself, at least once a month he recommended, and with that he was gone. Nicholas offered to accompany me back to my apartment. We left his place and headed back for Central Park, which surprisingly wasn't as far away as I would have imagined, and from there we headed through a small alleyway and came across a locked gate.

'Have you got the key?' I asked.

'I don't need it.' Nicholas told me.

I watched as Nicholas waved his hands slowly around the keyhole, clockwise.

'If you ever come across a locked door again, you can channel your magic to gently turn the lock,' He explained, 'Obviously only for purposes that are good!'

'Oh, now you've just killed my dream of becoming a seasoned criminal!' I looked at him with a dead expression, before laughing at the mock look of shock on his face.

Once we were through the door we continued out of the other side of the alley and found ourselves at the top of my street. I made a mental note of this new, easy access to the Other World from my new home as we walked quietly to my front door.

'Will I see you soon?' Nicholas asked, kissing me.

'Yes, when are you free?'

'The weekend?'

'Great! I'm going to see Martha and my Mammy over the next couple of days, make the most of my time off courtesy of Malachy's doctors note, but I'll head back on Friday.' I told him.

'Ok, I'll meet you here on Friday evening then, and we can see what we want to do.'

'Sounds like a plan, see you Friday.' I kissed him again.

'I'll miss you…' He muttered shyly.

'I'll miss you too!' I nodded, and we both smiled.

This was starting to get serious for us both, and in that moment, I felt us both realising it.

26 GOING HOME PART 2

I wondered around the apartment a little bit lost after Nicholas had left. Although I'd only been gone a few days it suddenly seemed a little unrecognisable. A bit like when you go on holiday and come home, and things look the same but feel a little different. It probably didn't help that I hadn't lived there long, but I couldn't settle at all. Bronagh was out, her sister still hadn't moved in, so there was just me wondering around trying to decide what to do with myself. I called Mammy and told her I was going to do a day trip the next day, and then I called Martha to arrange to see her. I asked to go that afternoon, but she was busy. I told her I was going to see Mammy the next day and Martha asked if she could come too, as she was up that way this evening and staying overnight at her friend's house. She offered to pick me up from the Train Station and drive us to Mammy's, so I agreed and hung up after only a couple of minutes on the phone. I hadn't killed much time and was pacing around trying to busy myself when I heard the door knock. I opened it apprehensively, not many people knew where I lived yet so I guessed it could only be the postman, but I was surprised to see Ethel standing there.

'Hi Gemma, how are you?'

'Hi Ethel, lovely to see you!' I spoke earnestly.

'I heard somebody moving about upstairs and I wanted to drop off some homemade fruit cake, fresh out of the oven! I hope I haven't interrupted…' She trailed off.

'Not at all, thank you so much!'

'I usually have to cut Gerald a slice first, but he's not home so you've got the best bit from the end!' She smiled proudly.

'That sounds great. Why don't you come in and have some with me, with a cup of Tea?'

'Ooh I wouldn't want to keep you from your busy day.'

'You wouldn't be. In fact, you would be doing me a favour. I've not been well and I'm better now but still having to rest a bit, and I'd love some company?' I almost pleaded with her.

'Ah well, if you're sure?' Ethel still stood hesitantly so I moved my body over to allow her in and gestured her through.

Ethel knew where she was going, it was her apartment after all, but she still stood nervously awaiting instruction from me on where to go. I directed her into the living room and told her to take a seat whilst I boiled the kettle. I cut 2 slices of the cake and allowed myself a second to indulge in the aroma that you only get from a freshly baked cake. It was delicious to the taste too, a proper homemade fruit cake that I hadn't had anything like since Granny used to make it. I quickly made the Tea and put everything on top of the tray, which I sat down on the coffee table, in the middle of our Lounge.

'Here we go.' I handed Ethel her Tea and cake.

'Thank you dear. So how are you finding things here? I do hope you like it?' Ethel enquired.

'We love it, honestly. We couldn't be happier! I hope you've not been disturbed by us being here?' I enquired back.

'Not at all. You are lovely girls, and so respectful. Exactly the type of tenants we wanted.'

I smiled at Ethel in response, but I couldn't resist the temptation of the cake any longer, so I took a huge great bite of it. The warm, sweet sensation filled my mouth like nothing I'd eaten before and I 'uhmmed' before I realised I was doing it. I barely noticed Ethel put her tea and cake down and start to wring her hands in agitation.

'I was hoping to see you on your own actually.' Ethel started.

'Mmm hmm…' I nodded, mouth and head still full of cake.

'It's just that, there's something about you that seems familiar?' Ethel half asked and I looked at her in surprise.

'What kind of familiar?' I asked, I wasn't sure what I could and couldn't say at this point without breaking the rules, Ethel had caught me off guard and I hadn't had chance to check with anyone.

'Well, I get a feeling that I know you.'

'You do?'

'I do. Like we might have met before, or have something in common?' Ethel stuttered, clearly not sure what to say either.

'Something in common like we've lived on the same street before, or something in common like we have similar knowledge and thoughts on things?' I queried, instantly wondering if I'd gone too far.

'Like we have similar knowledge. Like I know what you're about, and you know what I'm about?' Ethel braved to go further too.

'I think, in that case, we must both know 'Other' interesting things about each other.' I winked, still a little unsure but quietly confident I'd given a bold enough clue without disclosing anything I shouldn't.

'And 'Other' places we might have been to?!' Ethel winked back.

'Oh Ethel, this is amazing news!' I stood up and hugged her.

'I wasn't sure when we first met, but both Gerald and I knew that something had drawn us to your response to our Ad for the apartment. And when we met, I had a strong sense about you, but I wasn't sure if you knew it yet.'

'I'm so relieved, I can let my guard down a bit. I did feel a strange sensation when you gave me the pen and I too wondered about it. But I'm quite new to it all so wasn't sure how I could find out.' I explained.

'Yes, I felt that too! Gerald is from the Other World also, but I'm feeling that Bronagh is not?'

'No, sadly I don't think she is.' I shrugged.

'That's not to say she never will be dear.'

'I hope so Ethel, she'd love it so much. I hate keeping secrets from her too.'

'She has the ability within her. Her magic isn't as strong as yours, but she has it there if she chooses one day.'

'Fingers crossed she does – so what's your magic?' I asked

eagerly.

'I can sense people's abilities.' Ethel told me.

'Ah, I met a lady in the bookstore that does that too – amazing.'

'Enid Birchall, by any chance?'

'She was called Mrs Birchall…'

'That's my sister! We are twins, and we share the same ability. She's better than me though!'

'No way!' I was taken aback momentarily, 'But you don't look alike?'

'No, we're non-identical. She got the brains, and I got the beauty.' Ethel laughed.

'That's amazing. What about Gerald?'

'He didn't get either!' Ethel roared with laughter, and I giggled too.

I loved this newly discovered cheeky side to Ethel.

'Ah now, I think Gerald is very beautiful!' I teased.

'He is rather handsome,' She blushed, 'But his ability is Sight. He can see things, mostly in his mind but sometimes physically too.'

'How cool. How does it work?'

'He see's things in his mind, usually premonitions about things close to him that are major events. He worked hard on his abilities so that he can also concentrate on something intently, that might not be linked to him, and still see what happened if it's passed. He has, on occasion, seen something physically before him right before it has happened too. We were walking down the street one day and he saw a car mount the pavement. Gerald screamed at everyone to move and as people started to flee a car proceeded to mount the pavement where they had been. He saved so many lives.'

'Gosh, that is amazing.'

'It is indeed, and a bit scary at times.'

'It's so useful for him though. I bet he can do so much good with it?'

'Yes indeed. He spent all of his career working for Magic Intelligence, to help keep The Magicus Society safe, and also help solve serious crimes. He is very highly thought of in our World.'

'Wow, I can't believe that I've managed to move in with someone so talented.' I was awestruck.

I had so many questions but just then we heard the key turn in the lock and the door open and close, then in walked Bronagh.

'Ah, the patient!' She teased when she saw me, and then, 'Hi Ethel.' As she saw our guest.

'Hello dear.' Ethel smiled as she stood.

'You're not leaving, are you?' Bronagh asked.

'I am. I must get on, but I've left some cake for you.' Ethel told her.

'Yesssss, thank you!' Bronagh couldn't hide her delight.

'It was so lovely talking to you Ethel.' I told her with complete sincerity.

'You too dear, do come and visit us whenever you like girls. We love the company.'

'Will do.' I told her with a knowing smile, and waved goodbye as Ethel headed back down the stairs.

Bronagh chewed my ear off for the next half an hour, filling me in on everything that had been happening whilst I had been gone but I kept thinking about Ethel and Gerald, and how my feeling about them had been right. I was pleased with myself that my feeling sense was starting to gain some traction now I'd been working on it. I couldn't wait to put it to the test again, and I also couldn't wait for my next catch up with Ethel to learn more. As Bronagh neared the end of her gossiping I made my excuses and headed to my bedroom. The more I talked about magic, and absorbed myself in the Other World, the more I wanted to learn so I spent the rest of the evening in my room reading quietly.

The next morning, I got up early and headed out for my train. The train wasn't too busy, and I found a seat easily at a table. My plan was to do some University work, but as the train pulled out of the station I decided to read something light hearted to give my mind a break from all of the information I had garnered in the last few days, and try to refresh my brain away from thoughts of magic so I would be ready to get back to thoughts of my studies. We weren't long into the journey when I heard the ticket inspector coming around. As he called out and moved further down the carriage towards me, I noticed a young Mother with a small child keep moving seats whenever the conductor was busy looking at each ticket. I knew instantly that she hadn't paid her fare and could see the fear in her eyes. Unfortunately, the ticket inspector saw her too, and bellowed at her to stay put as he marched down the carriage until he was right in front of her.

'Do you have the correct ticket Mam?' He almost shouted at her.

Her eyes started to fill with tears, as she pretended to be hunting around for a ticket.

'Do you have any ticket at all?' He bellowed again.

Tears started to stream down her face as she gave up the pretense of looking for a ticket and hung her head low.

'Mam, may I remind you that it is an offence to travel on a public train with no ticket. Now I will ask again, do you have a ticket?'

The conductor was aggressive and harsh, and his loud voice had caused several people around the carriage to stop what they were doing and watch the scene he was creating begin to unfold. My heart broke for this young girl, who was clearly very upset by the incident.

'I'm so sorry, I couldn't afford one.' She cried out.

'But yet you thought it was ok to travel. That is was ok for all of these passengers around you to pay the fare, but you not to?' He almost growled as he spoke low and angrily.

'No, I didn't think that. But I needed to get back to my Mom and Dad's, to get my baby to safety from his aggressive Dad, but I have no money.' She looked down at her small child who also started to cry at the angry man shouting at his Mom.

'Well what a shame. But the law is the law!' The conductor spoke with utter sarcasm.

'I'll pay her fare.' Another passenger offered.

The girl smiled gratefully, but this just seemed to irritate the conductor more.

'Unfortunately, that isn't enough…' He smirked, 'I must also issue her with a £90 fine.'

'Oh, now come on,' An elderly woman interjected, 'Is that really necessary?'

'I'm just doing my job. I mustn't let freeloaders off scot free or they'll all be at it. Chancing their luck.'

'But you can clearly see she's upset, and desperate!' I pleaded for her.

'Desperate doesn't pay to run this train.' He shot me an evil glance and rage boiled inside me.

As the other passengers tried to defend the young girl, I willed with everything I had that the conductor would relent and show leniency. I stared hard at him and I could feel all of my angry will bubbling deep inside of me. I wasn't an aggressive person, but I felt almost a boiling rage at the lack of compassion from this man, and desperately hoped he would relent in his excessive force towards the young, terrified

Mother.

The conductor was almost finished with writing the fine out when he paused, and a confused look spread across his face. The young Mom, and her son, were almost hysterically crying now and a group of passengers had formed a small crowd around her to comfort her and offer her bits of money to help with the fine. As the conductor looked around, he caught my eye with his and I threw every ounce of compassion I could at him in one last attempt. He lingered a moment longer before he cleared his throat and spoke.

'Ok, I will let the fine go this time…' He continued to speak but I didn't hear him. Relief washed over the face of the young girl almost in unison to the feeling of encouragement and surprise I felt brewing inside of me. I had done it. For the first time ever, I had moved my feeling in to someone else. After all of my studying, I had finally been able to use my magic for something good, and I couldn't have felt prouder.

27 HOME

As I exited the train station a small car raced up beside me, almost swiping my arm, and Martha frantically waved out of the window to me. Several people turned to look at us due to Martha's unorthodox driving, but Martha didn't seem to notice the head shakes and tutting that was being thrown her way. I was still shaking from the experience on the train, so I didn't much care about the looks we were getting either, I just waved back with a wilted smile and jumped on in.

'Thanks for this Martha.'

'Of course, dear, thanks for having me. I'm so excited to see your Mam, and this is the first time I've seen you two together since you both found out about each other so it will be a great visit!' Martha was filled with enthusiasm.

'Well it's actually only the second time I've seen her since we've found out.' I smiled.

'There should be lots for us to talk about then!'

The drive home was quick and filled with light chat, mostly from Martha. I tried to distract myself in the small talk, although I desperately wanted to tell her what I'd done. But I wanted to tell Mammy too, so I bit my tongue and waited until we'd arrived. Mammy was stood waiting for us on the doorstep, as we pulled up, and her face showed that she was delighted to have us arrive. Now that I knew about Mammy's magic, I had started to look at her in a whole new light. As Martha proceeded to edge the car backwards and forwards, slowly manoeuvring the car closer to the kerb so it sat just right, I used the time to admire how well Mammy was put together. She had always been like this, as far back as I could remember. Aside from the perfectly ironed ensemble, which I now knew had a little help from Mammy's Other skills, I noted that her hair and makeup were always perfect too. I mean, they *always* were. Her hair, usually pinned back, never had but a wisp out of place. And her red lipstick, that she wore every day without fail, never seemed to rub away or smudge. I thought of all the little magical tricks she used in the house and started to wonder. Maybe she could teach me to incorporate a little bit of Other ability in my look too? I'd have to ask her, I thought as Martha finally pulled the handbrake up dramatically in a kind of 'ta-da' that she was finally done parking. Mammy rushed out to the car and embraced us one by one, as tightly as she could.

'I'm so happy that you're both here!' Mammy declared.

'I'm delighted that you asked me.' Martha told her.

'I'm so happy to be here with you both too!' I told them warmly, 'And I've got something to tell you both!'

'Ooh, go on then!' Mammy smiled whilst Martha eyed me playfully.

'Let's go inside first.' I instructed.

Once we'd settled inside with a pot of tea and a slice of toast – that Mammy had insisted on – I regaled the whole train tale. Mammy and Martha sat perfectly quiet, listening, whilst uhhming and ahhing in all the right places.

'Gemma, that is amazing – Well Done you!' Martha smiled at

me.

'Thank you. Obviously I would never try to influence anyone for the wrong reason, and I won't be making a habit out of it as I appreciate it is a very personal thing to tamper with, but I'm so happy I was able to help that young girl and her baby get away without the fine. She clearly was desperate and wasn't trying to be malicious.'

'Of course, she wasn't, and it sounds like the ticket inspector needed a little compassion – especially after that other passenger had offered to pay her fare, just let it go!' Mammy shook her head crossly.

'It's a credit to you that you were able to help her Gemma, clearly you've been working hard at your magic.' Martha nodded encouragingly.

'I have. I love it. I have this thirst for more knowledge, I can't get enough!'

'Well, I was thinking… how about the three of us visit the Other World today?' Mammy asked cautiously.

Martha and I looked at each other in surprise and turned to face Mammy.

'But Mam, I thought that you didn't want to go again as you didn't like keeping secrets from Daddy?!'

'Ah well, I did used to feel like that. But that was before, when you didn't know either. I didn't want to have another life that my family knew nothing about. I felt like I would be the same as those people who cheat and have secret families on the side. You hear about it all the time, then years later the wives and children find out that they've got girlfriends and kids somewhere else, and they spend all the time there when they said they were working overtime!'

'I think you've been watching too much daytime TV!' Martha and I giggled in unison, and Mammy smiled back at us.

'Well you know what I mean. I didn't want to live two lives, and that's how I felt it would be at the time. But I would like to go back, for old times' sake. Not to stay, or keep visiting, just as a one off.'

'And Daddy?' I asked.

'I'll just tell him Martha drove us to the Village up the way, for something different to do.'

'Right well, I'm in. Let's go!' Martha stood, and beckoned us up.

We left the house and headed across the street and into the wooded area I used to play in as a child. It was a quiet day, and we didn't see any of the neighbours around as we walked, which wasn't unusual but nonetheless felt like a welcome relief. Mammy instructed us on which way to go all of the way there, and I felt a sentimental sense of familiarity as I looked around and remembered all of the fun and games we used to have in these woods as children.

'My favourite tree is up here.' I proudly told Mammy and Martha.

'Oh yes?' Martha questioned, 'And how have you got a favourite tree?'

'From when I was a child. It is amazing. A huge great thing, so old but so grand. We loved playing on it as kids, we always headed to it. It was kind of spooky, and we believed that the witch might live in there. Ha, hours we'd spend there, convinced it held some kind of magic…' I trailed off as we reached the tree and stood in front of it adoringly, as Mammy cleared her throat.

'Oh, but Gemma, it does.'

Both Martha and I turned to Mammy for some elaboration, but she didn't seem to notice as she continued to wonder at the tree and walk towards it. The roots of the tree stuck out from the ground somewhat, and as they twisted and turned up and down, they were almost as tall as we were. Mammy continued to walk until she was in the heart of the roots and then bent down and started to crawl underneath one of them. Martha and I looked at each other but without any words being needed we knew that this was a gateway to the other world. We immediately followed Mammy, and I couldn't believe that we had never found this as children. Mammy continued to crawl underneath the roots until we were completely inside the tree. Then she pushed at a tiny handle, that was difficult to see in the dark with the naked eye and opened the door to the Other World. As we all emerged, we brushed ourselves down, as we were covered in dirt, and Mammy started to speak.

'Not the most glamorous of the entrances!' She declared, 'But does the job.'

'I've never used that one before, but I do recall Elsie telling me all about it. She would wear protective clothing when she came through, is that the one?' Martha asked.

'Haha,' Mammy chuckled, 'Yes that's right, she would. I'd forgotten about that!'

'At least it's not a wet day, so nothing that can't be brushed off today.' Martha exclaimed.

'How have I never found that as a child?' I wondered aloud.

'You were probably always with your friends Gemma. Plus, I bet you'd never ventured quite that far inside… they don't make it easy for a reason!' Mammy told me.

'No, we probably hadn't gone that deep inside,' I was stood in astonishment, 'It's no wonder it felt special to me though.'

'Right, what do you want to do?' Martha asked us both.

'This is Mammy's day,' I grinned to her, 'You choose.'

'Well, there's this great cookery school I used to go to, but it's in Other Thailand?' Mammy half asked.

'A cookery school?' Martha frowned, clearly not phased about the Thailand part.

'It's fantastic Martha. The woman who runs it is a real hoot. It's full on crazy, in your face magical fun… it's actually her that the story of Mary Poppins was based on.'

Mammy was so full of hope and enthusiasm that neither Martha nor I could refuse.

'Let's go!' I grinned.

Getting to Other Thailand was just as easy as getting to Other Netherlands. We queued at our terminal, walked through one set of doors and out through another and there we were, on a breath-taking beach in Thailand.

'Well, it was worth coming for the scenery alone!' Martha declared, and Mammy and I both nodded in agreement.

There was perfect white sand as far as the eye could see, with glistening turquoise water running alongside it in perfect harmony. All across the top of the beach stood various huts serving up authentic street food, but Mammy gestured up the beach and informed us this was the way we were going. We strolled up the beach slowly, taking in the wonderful surroundings. There were many people around, mostly tourists enjoying the blistering hot sun whilst they relaxed on a sun lounger, with a few locals around trying to convince the tourists to buy an excursion, some food or whatever they had on them to sell. There were a couple of small wooden boats pulled half on to the shore and I could see that these were being rented out, and I made a mental note to bring Nicholas back here for a romantic boat ride. Further up the beach stood some rock faces, and Mammy informed us that it was within these that we were heading.

As soon as we arrived, I could see how the idea of Mary Poppins came from this lady, and also why Mammy described it as full on magic. An old woman stood in the middle of the room shouting instructions to a room full of students, whilst pots and pans whizzed through the air, moving from the place they'd been shelved to the person that needed to cook with them. As students called out for more ingredients, these too were sent flying through the air by the enchanting teacher and dropped down in front of the student. I'd never seen anything quite like it and stood with my mouth agape.

'It's much quicker to move them around this way!' The teacher told me, having noticed my stunned expression, 'Come, find a bench!' She instructed.

We wondered in and managed to find some bench space together. The place was filled with noise. Chatter, music, the teacher shouting instructions. I had to hand it to Mammy, it was truly wonderful. I wasn't that interested in the cooking, and from Martha's expression when Mammy first mentioned it, I assumed she wasn't either, but we both looked around in enthusiastic wonder. Straight away Mammy started calling out for the tools and ingredients she needed and picked up instructions quickly. Martha and I hesitated a little but soon joined in. I found, once I'd got over the shock of it, I loved having everything I needed fly through the air and come to me just like how I'd imagined magic to be when I was a small child. I even enjoyed the cooking part of the class. If I undercooked something, I could merely tell it to be more cooked and it was. Likewise, if I burned something, I could instruct it to undo the burn and it would. The place was unapologetically mad, but Mammy had been right, it used magic to the extreme.

Martha struggled a little more with the cooking side of it, in particular she found the Papaya difficult to deal with.

'Oh, you stupid food!' She cried as she tussled with it whilst trying to cut it up.

The Papaya suddenly sprung to life and jumped up, spraying seeds in her face, before laying back down lifeless again.

'You need to respect the food!' The teacher shouted across, 'Treat it badly and it will treat you badly.'

Mammy and I chuckled as Martha whispered an apology to the fruit, and then muttered under her breath that she'd never heard anything like having to be respectful of fruit. After that she did seem to relax and get into it, and by the end of her lesson she'd made the most delicious looking Thai Papaya Salad. I had gone a bit wilder and made Pad Thai, whilst Mammy had made a type of Thai curry called Panang. We all looked at our dishes with great pride and boxed them up to take with us to eat whilst thanking the teacher and telling her what a wonderful cookery school she had.

After we'd left, Mammy showed us to a peaceful spot on the beach for us to eat our creations. It was a small alcove, just down from the cookery school but out of viewpoint for tourists, and there was nothing else there apart from us and a small swing that sat up high over the water. As we sat down and tucked in to our food Mammy told us that she would often come here in the past as a way to unwind when she needed time to think, and she would enjoy the wacky cooking class and then sit on the swing and enjoy the view until she felt her mind clear. We finished our food, and each had a turn in sitting on the swing and enjoying the healing effects that Mammy had described. It was an incredible feeling moving backwards and forwards, over the sea, looking out on to such a wonderful view and feeling the breeze across the skin bringing some welcome relief from the blazing sun. I knew, before we'd left, that I would be coming back here. And I guessed Martha would too. As the heat started to become less intense, we decided to head back so that we could get Mammy back before Daddy got home, and he would be none the wiser.

'Thank you for a marvelous experience!' Martha hugged Mammy as we were saying our goodbyes on her doorstep.

'It was truly the best day I could have asked for.' I agreed, also taking a turn to give Mammy a tight hug.

'Thank you both. It's been a long time since I've been to that place, and I think about it often. Now I've had this experience, I feel I can go another 20 years before I need to go back!' Mammy giggled.

'I think I need 20 years before I go back and face the aggressive fruit!' Martha declared, but chuckled.

'That literally made my day!' I laughed as Martha teasingly gave me an evil eye.

'Please do come and visit me again soon?' Mammy asked us both.

'We definitely will.' We both promised her.

The drive home was long, we hit rush hour traffic and it is not an easy thing to maneuver through in Central London. We spent most of the journey talking about our wonderful day, the crazy experience, and how great it was that Mammy allowed herself to go back. I told Martha I couldn't wait to remake my recipe, and she told me she couldn't wait to order hers in a Thai restaurant. We laughed and joked about life, but as we neared home a strange feeling niggled inside me. It was minor at first, and I wondered if it might be an adverse reaction to the food or the journey. But the closer we got to home, the stronger it became, until there was no denying that it was a feeling of uneasiness in the pit of my stomach. I knew that it meant something wasn't right, but I had no idea what could be causing it as we'd had a fantastic day out. We turned the corner into the street behind Martha's, that housed the garage at the end of her garden, and I had a flashback of when I had turned up at her house that day with the bad feelings. Was this a throwback of that? Had the protection spell not worked properly? Maybe it was being back at Martha's that served as a reminder? But as we exited the garage and into her house, I suddenly realised what it was, I remembered.

'Martha…' I started cautiously, afraid of what she may be about to tell me.

'Yes dear?' she was distracted by some post and didn't look at me, which made it a little easier to ask.

'When I came here last week, you said something that's been bothering me…'

'I did?'

'Yes. When you were trying to find out what was wrong with me initially you asked me if I was upset about a girl… a girl called Everly.'

'I did.' She nodded.

'Who is she? Should I know her?'

'I thought you did know her?'

'Well I do know an Everly. Very briefly. I met her in the park one day, and I saw her another day when I was with Nicholas…' Dread filled the pit of my stomach as I said it, 'It was a bit strange actually. But should I know her?'

'I'm sorry Gemma, I assumed you knew. She's Nicholas ex-Girlfriend.'

28 TELL ME ALL

Almost half an hour later I arrived at Nicholas house, just as dusk had set and darkness was all around. I could see Nicholas house lit up in the distance, so I knew he was home. As I approached his gate, I felt sick with nerves and hesitated slightly. Martha had explained to me how Nicholas and Everly had been in a long-term relationship, but Nicholas had called it off about 6 months ago. Apparently Everly was struggling to get over it and seemed to be stalking Nicholas, constantly turning up when he was working or out with friends. Martha had heard through Gabriel about how Everly had appeared in the park that day, when we were on a date, and Nicholas had later gone to confront her over it. Gabriel thought Nicholas had told me, so Martha had assumed that day when I turned up upset it was because of Everly.

I walked tentatively through the front gate and onto the path. I could see Wilfred asleep in his flower and watched him for a while, so peaceful and unassuming. Tears brimmed at my eyes as I thought about all I had learned from Nicholas. What if me coming here caused a big argument and Nicholas and I ended up going our separate ways? I might never see Wilfred again. Would I ever find someone who was as patient and helpful with my learning as Nicholas was? Would I be able to even come back to the Other World now that I'd been made a fool of? But the biggest fear of all was if I would ever be able to get over Nicholas… However, I knew deep down that I couldn't just forget about this, like I did that day in the park, and act like nothing had happened. As much as I longed to unknow what I now knew, I knew that this wasn't possible – I had even checked with Martha if there was a spell to make me forget.

But sadly not. I raised my hand and gently knocked at the door. I was flooded with emotion, and secretly hoped that Nicholas wouldn't open the door. But as I was about to turn and walk away the door widened and Nicholas stood in the light.

As soon as I looked into Nicholas eyes I burst into floods of tears. Nicholas ushered me inside and wrapped me tight in his arms. I sobbed for a few minutes, while he stood in silence gently stroking my hair. Moments later, as my tiredness grew, and my tears slowed Nicholas gently released me and guided me through to the living room and on to the sofa. Still without saying a word, Nicholas wondered into the kitchen and returned with a large glass of wine for me and a beer for him. He sat next to me and held me once more.

'I'm so sorry Gemma, I should have told you what was going on.' He spoke.

I didn't speak for a while. Instead I tried to compose myself a little, sitting upright and sipping at my wine trying to use the sharpness to distract myself from the ache in my heart and head, and therefore stop the tears. It seemed to work, and for a while I just felt numb with confusion.

'Gemma, please speak to me.' Nicholas pleaded, gently holding my hand.

'Did you cheat on me with her?' I asked slowly and boldly.

'No Gemma, of course I didn't!' Nicholas almost shouted in response.

'So, what happened that night you went to see her… Why

didn't you tell me like you told Gabriel you were going to?' I turned to look him in the eye.

'I should have. I was just scared.'

'Of what? If you hadn't done anything wrong what were you scared of?'

'You walking away from me.' It was his turn to divert his eyes to the floor, as I had done when I first arrived.

'Why would I do that?'

'Because I've got a psycho ex-girlfriend following me around who will do anything in her power to cause trouble between us – it's hardly worth the effort for you is it!'

I couldn't see Nicholas face well now, despite his head hanging so low, and I could see that he too had tears filling his eyes.

'And that's it… that's the only reason I'd have to walk away from you?' I spoke a little more gently now.

'Of course. Gemma, I'd never do anything to hurt you.' Nicholas looked back up and met my eyes, and we both started to cry again, but a softer cry this time.

We sat on the sofa for a while, cuddling, not saying anything. Every so often Nicholas would kiss me on the head, in a sign of affection.

'I wouldn't walk away from you because of that!' I broke the silence, 'But I am so hurt that you didn't feel you could trust me. That you let me find out this way.'

'Gemma, I'm mortified that you have found out like this. I

really am. I was going to tell you, I promise. I just couldn't find the right time. We were having so much fun, and you were enjoying the Other World so much I didn't want to taint that for you.'

'Didn't you think I'd find out?'

'Of course, I did. I thought you'd find out from me. I promise, I was just searching for the right time to talk to you about it. It has weighed down so heavy on me, especially since I met you. I just didn't want to scare you away.'

'I feel like a fool that all of these other people have been talking about it, and me, behind my back.'

'Gemma, it isn't like that. I've only spoken to Gabriel about it because I asked him to cover my shift whilst I went to confront Everly. I was so angry after she approached us that day in the park, and I had to go and tell her it needed to stop. I haven't spoken to another soul about it, I wouldn't do that to you!'

'So, what did she say, when you went to see her?'

'She said she wants to be with me. She doesn't want anyone else to be with me.'

'She's not going to stop her pursuit of you?'

Nicholas wiped his eyes and run his fingers through his hair clearly exasperated.

'No, she's not. I don't know what to do. That's why I didn't want to tell you, because I can't see that it's going to get any better. I just don't know what to do!'

I looked at Nicholas' red, tear streamed face and felt the uneasiness within me melt away. He was telling the truth and I knew it. I thought for a moment, about the amazing time I'd had with Nicholas, and how happy he had been making me. Did I want to throw all of that away? The thought of dealing with a woman that was clearly obsessed did make me nervous. I had never been a confrontational person, and I didn't want to become one. But I didn't want to give up on my new relationship either.

'Nicholas be honest with me now. Are you happy with me?'

'Happier than I've been in a long time.' Nicholas still didn't raise his head.

'Do you promise that from now on you will be completely honest with me, about everything?'

'Of course – I swear to you that I will never hide anything from you again!' He looked at me this time, eyes pleading.

'I think, if we both really want to continue in this relationship, that we can overcome an ex-Girlfriend following us around. But we both have to really want it….'

'Do you really want it?' He asked me cautiously.

'I do,' I nodded and looked deep into his eyes, 'Do you?'

'Gemma, I….. I love you.'

I sat momentarily and stared blankly at Nicholas. It took a few moments for his words to sink in, he had caught me completely off guard and it took a few seconds for my mind to register the enormity of what he'd said.

'You love me?' I asked slowly.

'I know its soon Gemma, and I don't want to frighten you off, but I wanted to tell you so that you know that I'm serious about you. About us!'

'But you love me?' I was still a little dumbfounded.

'Yes!' Nicholas mouth curled slightly at the edges in amusement, 'I love you! I don't expect you to say it back or anything…'

'I love you too!' I butted in.

'You do?'

'I do. I really do!' And with that I kissed Nicholas hard.

I knew it was soon, but I also knew what I felt. Nicholas was sexy, funny, kind. He was everything I never believed I could find in a partner, and although I was inexperienced in the love department, I was sure of what I felt. Everything felt right, comfortable. I wasn't the kind of person to go out and have one-night stands, or short flings, nor did I want to be that person. I was happy with Nicholas, and he was obviously happy with me, and I felt deep inside that this was right between us.

The rest of the evening passed in a bit of a blur. After the initial euphoria and act of lust we curled up together in bed and talked into the early hours. We talked about Everly, and what she was trying to do. Nicholas agreed to tell me anything that happened from now on, and I promised I would let him know if she made contact with me. Nicholas explained that when he went to see Everly he made it quite clear that she would never change his mind about them. If anything, she had just made it clearer that she would never be an option for him. Everly didn't take it well and promised him that she would not allow him to be happy and would make it her mission to split him up from me, and any other girlfriends he may have. I asked Nicholas if he were worried that she would fulfil her promise, but he seemed sure that she would get bored eventually, especially if she met someone else, and would give up on him. He did, however, believe that she would stay intent on splitting us up, at least for now, and he suspected that she would target me on my own next. Perhaps try to befriend me and make up some tales about him to put me off.

'You must trust your feelings Gemma, whatever I or anyone else tells you, your feelings will always lead you to the truth.'

I felt a little relieved in the knowledge that I had built my feeling sense up and I now knew that I could always rely on it to help me find the truth.

'Do you think if we spent more time in the Real World she will stay away, with her living in the Other World?' I asked hopefully.

'Unlikely,' Nicholas replied, 'She's got family in the Real World. It's where she grew up. She wouldn't be afraid to spend more time in the Real World.'

'It was just a thought. What's her magical sense?'

'She has the movement sense. She can make things move with her mind. It's not strong, she's not very good at it. She couldn't make something move if it wasn't right in front of her, or if it were large or heavy.'

'So, no immediate threat with any mind or feeling games?'

'No. Nothing that I can think of. She might throw things at us in the park.' Nicholas laughed.

'It's not funny!' I giggled along, 'What have I got myself into?'

'A loving relationship!'

29 WE'RE IN THIS TOGETHER

The next morning, I woke up to find Nicholas curled tightly around me. I was happier than I'd ever been, and I was certain that I wouldn't let anyone else ruin it. I also realised that, for the first time, I truly understood Mammy's decision to leave behind her Other life to be with Daddy, the man she loved and had committed to. I didn't know if I would be with Nicholas forever, but I did know that right now I would do everything necessary to keep us together. I kissed the tip of his nose and felt him stir.

'Morning love of my life!' He grinned cheekily at me.

'Morning my handsome love.' I gave him an animated wink that had him laughing a big, carefree belly laugh which made my heart soar.

'Well, I'm afraid to tell you I have plans today.'

'You do?' I eyed him questioningly.

'Yeah – I'm sorry. I'm meeting the lads for a few beers. Shall I cancel? I can cancel and we can do something?'

'No, go! Who are these lads?'

'A group of lads that I've been friends with since I was a kid. Some of them live here full time, some of them just visit, but we've all been coming to the Other World with our parents since young so we kind of bonded over our mutual secret!' He stood and grabbed a towel to head to the shower.

'That's lovely, I hope you enjoy!'

'Why don't you come?' He asked me seriously.

'Ah I wouldn't want to impose!'

'You wouldn't be imposing. They'd love to meet you, and I'd love you to meet them. If you feel comfortable going?'

'Are you sure they wouldn't mind?'

'Of course, they wouldn't. But how about I'll tell them you've come for one drink, and if after that you want to go then I'll walk you back to your exit home and head back to them on my own? That way you can stay if you want to or go after one drink without needing to find an excuse?'

'Ok, that sounds great. I'm looking forward to meeting your friends.... I was starting to think you didn't have any.' I teased, smirking.

'I am a bit of a loner!' Nicholas chuckled as he headed out of the room to the shower, before we dressed and headed out.

Nicholas was right, his friends were so pleased to meet me and welcome me in for a drink. They were all lovely too and made me feel so comfortable and at ease in their company.

'So, Gemma, tell us... is Nick the big, soppy romantic we think he is?' His friend Jack teased.

'Absolutely!' I nodded, making him blush a little as they all roared with laughter.

'Probably needs to be now he's punching above his weight!' Another of his friends Tim nudged him in the ribs laughing.

'I certainly am punching.' Nicholas nodded and winked at me.

'Ah look at him, all mushy eyed!' Tim poked fun at him.

'And mushy bellied!' His friend Gerry interjected, 'He's clearly been neglecting the gym!'

We all roared with laughter once again.

'Right, enough about me!' Nicholas demanded light heartedly, whilst mockingly pulling his t-shirt down further.

'Tell us about you lovely Gemma!' Gerry asked.

'What do you want to know?'

'Where do you live? Where are you from? How did you come to be here? How did you end up with this lucky bugger?'

I launched into my spiel, telling Nicholas friends all about me and my background. They seemed genuinely interested and asked lots of questions making me feel extremely relaxed in their company. One drink turned in to three, and I not only told them all about me, I also learned all about them. I could tell by the way they gently spoke about Nicholas that they were extremely fond and protective of him. It was lovely to hear and to see the bond that they all had. They filled me with stories about Nicholas from his childhood and adolescent, and frequently mocked him in a good-natured manner. They all seemed extremely close, and I loved this support network that Nicholas had built up around him. After we'd all finished our third drink it was Nicholas turn to get a round in, and he gestured for me to come with him.

'No way!' Jack told him, 'She's staying with us. We need to find out some of your secrets.'

We all chuckled, and Nicholas hesitantly walked off into the pub.

'He's a really good guy Gemma.' Gerry told me as soon as Nicholas was out of earshot.

'The best!' Tim agreed.

'He's had a tough time these last few years, but he's seemed so different since meeting you.' Jack nodded encouragingly.

'Good, I'm glad!' I smiled.

'And we're glad for you both, you seem really happy together – Welcome to the fold!' Gerry winked and they all gave me a little hug.

We stayed in the pub most of the afternoon, but slowly, one by one, all of Nicholas friends left to head back to their daily responsibilities until it was only the two of us left.

'Fancy some dinner at mine?' Nicholas asked.

'Have you not got work?' I queried.

'No, not tonight. I never work after meeting the lads, so I can have a few jars without worrying.'

'If you don't mind… or should I get home?'

'Have you got anything to get home for?'

'Not really.'

'That's settled that then.'

We strolled back to Nicholas house, hand in hand, laughing

about some of the stories his friends had told. In response, Nicholas filled me in on some of their misdemeanors and I could see that the last 24 hours had resulted in a calmness about Nicholas that made him so much more at ease with me. As we sat down for dinner, I knew it was the time to finally ask the question that had been bugging me recently.

'Nicholas, I don't mean to pry but I just wondered…' I hesitated.

'Where my parents are?' He trailed off.

'Well, yes. It's just that you talk about them a lot in your stories. It's fine if you don't want to tell me.'

'They passed away Gemma.'

Sadness dogged at Nicholas eyes.

'Oh Nicholas, I'm so sorry!'

'It's ok, you weren't to know. I should have broached the subject myself, but just like the Everly thing it's hard to know when the right time is, and what to say.'

'Please don't feel you need to explain, I'm not sure I would know what to say either.'

I moved around to Nicholas and encased him in my arms.

'I'm honestly so sorry I asked!' I spoke tenderly.

'It's ok, really. They were in a car accident in the Real World, a year ago now. I still lived there with them, and my sister, although they'd bought this place as a second home a long time before then. They were driving back from some friends one night when their car came off the road. They were both killed on impact. The police never got to the bottom of what happened.'

I felt Nicholas pain within me, and I longed to make it better for him. I held him tighter, and he returned my affection by clinging on to my arms.

'It's still quite raw, I'm not going to lie.' He shrugged.

'Of course, it is! I don't know what to say.'

'There's nothing to say. I will tell you all about them, but just not tonight if that's ok?'

'Whenever you're ready, I'll be there!' I kissed him delicately and gave him another squeeze.

He didn't mention his parents for the rest of the evening, and neither did I. After a minute of composing himself Nicholas went back to light-hearted chat, mostly about his friends and mine. We went to bed early, although I didn't sleep well. Nicholas was extremely restless and had some bad dreams which resulted in him shouting out a few times. I comforted him and stroked his head each time until he settled back down, but I found myself lay in the dark with a million thoughts running through my head. A lot had happened in the last couple of days. I felt fiercely protective of Nicholas now I knew all about what was going on with him, and I was determined to see Everly away. I would not let her ruin us. I would speak with Mammy and Martha, see if they could impart some words of wisdom on the situation. Heck, I might even speak with Bronagh. Obviously, I would need to omit all the magical references, but I could still give her a good overview of the ex-girlfriend stalking us. The only trouble would be that Bronagh would want to go and speak with her. Maybe I'd rethink about talking to her about it. As I thought about Bronagh I realised I missed her a little. I hadn't seen her much lately and I wanted to spend some time with her. But even just thinking about going back home brought back a familiar niggle in the pit of my stomach. Just like what I'd felt when I was with Martha. But all that Everly stuff is out in the open now, I thought. What could it be? As the night wore on it grew a little stronger each time I thought of going home. As morning dawned, I was ready to get up and head back. I had a feeling something bad was going to happen and I just wanted to go back and find out what it was, confront it head on. I felt sure nothing had happened to Bronagh, because she would have let me know, but even so, as soon as it was an acceptable time, I text her.

HI BRONAGH, EVERYTHING OK? X

I had a response almost immediately.

YES, FINE THANKS. WHEN YOU COMING BACK? X

I felt relief, but still I couldn't shake the bad feeling looming over me.

I'LL BE BACK THIS MORNING. WILL YOU BE THERE? X

I hoped she would. If something else bad had happened, back in the Real World, I wanted her support.

YES, SEE YOU IN A BIT. PICK UP MILK X

The tapping on my phone disturbed Nicholas and he rolled

over and looked up at me.

'You ok?' He squinted at me through tired eyes.

'Yes. I think so.' I lied.

'What's wrong?' His eyes opened wider now, with concern.

'Nothing, it's just a feeling.'

'A bad one?'

'Not really bad, but yeah. I'm going to go home, just make sure everything is ok.' I climbed out of bed.

'Yes sure, do you want me to come?' He asked filled with concern.

'No, it's fine. Bronagh is home anyway. You stay in bed and I'll call you later.'

'I don't mind coming with you?'

'No, honestly. I'll let you know what it is.'

'Ok. But come straight back here if you need to. Or phone me and I'll come to you… Promise me?'

'I promise!' I declared as I kissed him goodbye.

As I walked back to the exit of the Other World, I felt really strange. A really strong feeling of nerves had come over me, and my legs felt quite jelly like. I wasn't even sure I would be able to make it home at one point, and I stopped at a café I was passing for a cup of Tea and a sit down. I filled my Tea with sugar, even though I didn't usually take it, as people always swear by it being good for shock. But it did nothing to help me, and I knew I just needed to get home and face whatever was coming. I passed over to the Real World easily, but as soon as I'd crossed over a wave of nausea hit me and I almost felt scared to go home. Part of me wanted to turn and run back to the Other World, back to Nicholas, but I knew this feeling wouldn't go away and I needed to find out what was causing it so I could go about dealing with it. As I turned on to my street my legs felt heavy, like I was having to drag them along and I really wished I'd let Nicholas come with me. Bronagh will be home, I told myself, she can support me. Whatever it is, I can trust her to help. Even if it's something magical, I can twist the truth and talk to her, I told myself.

As I reached our entrance, I stood hesitantly looking at it. The feeling was so strong now that I knew whatever it was lay behind it. Surely it couldn't be to do with Bronagh, could it? She'd said everything was fine. I pushed my key in the lock and turned the handle slowly, scared to look inside and uncover what dreaded thing lay ahead. The door opened easily but I froze in horror as I stared inside.

'Gemma, you're home – I've missed you!' Bronagh declared, throwing her arms around me.

But I couldn't reciprocate. I was transfixed in trepidation at the figure stood ahead of me. She walked forward and smiled, and I had no idea what was happening. Was I dreaming? Is this real? But before I could process any more thoughts, Bronagh spoke again.

'Here she is Gemma, finally… Meet my sister, and our new flatmate…. Everly.'

ABOUT THE AUTHOR

Kerry lives in Stourbridge, West Midlands with her husband, two Daughters and Cat.